Rocks & Stones Between A Rose

Part 1

Smokey Moment

Become a Social Media Friend. Follow me on:

Twitter: smokeymomentbo1

Instagram: smokey.moment

Facebook: smokeymomentbooks

OR

Visit my website:

http://www.smokeymomentbooks.com

Acknowledgments

Dedicated to all the readers who love a good book that keeps you guessing, laughing, cursing, crying and all caught up in your emotions!

Table of Contents

Prologue

*I*t was a rainy afternoon. Rose glanced out of the window and sighed. She was still breathing at a fast pace. Her sex drive had amped up and her frustrations had grown. She had no one to make love to, but herself and it was nobody's fault but her own. Life had come full circle and she was staring at walls she shouldn't be.

This was her house, but it wasn't her home. She wasn't welcome at her home. She had done things that had torn a man and his family apart. Her high sex drive and inability to control it, had just caused her to lose a relationship envied by many. A relationship with a man most women would have adored. Rose laid there, hands down her panties, feeling the loss. She was wracked with guilt and she had regrets.

"What is wrong with me?" she thought, as she watched the rain hitting her window pane. Rose looked back to the ceiling then looked over near her bedroom door. Near the door was an oil painting. She'd hung the picture she found in a pile of old furniture from a renovated building. It *was a painting of a little girl wearing rubber boots, a rain coat and holding an umbrella.*

"I love that picture," she thought, as she stared at it. Rose couldn't help but notice how carefree the child looked as she played in the rain. She wondered what that little girls' life must be like. What's it like to live in a world with such happiness. "Who would enjoy the rain in such a way but a child whose world was secure, bright and full of life," she thought.

She imagined that the little girls' life must be complete with a mother and a father. Parents whose sole purpose in life was to nurture and care for their child. Rose wondered what her life would have been like if she'd had the same love and care. If there had been someone to nurture and care for her just like the child in the picture. Rose blamed her childhood troubles for her now adult problems. But Rose could have catapulted her way to the top regardless of her humble beginnings and troubled childhood.

She was a bombshell. A stunning beauty and everyone, including her own mother, wanted in. Just about everyone she came in contact with sought out a way to get closer to her. She had come full circle and couldn't help but wish she would have made better choices. Rose stood there recounting the series of events that lead her back to this place. Back to the house she'd left behind to live what she thought was a fabulous life. An envied life. It all started just a few years ago...

Chapter One – Rose

*R*ose hurried down the street. *Damn! I'm going to be late,* she said, as she ran towards the bus stop. She waved at the driver hoping he wouldn't keep going. He saw her running and waved back, as he pulled up to the stop. She thought about catching a cab, but saw the bus coming instead. Besides, cabs cost more and Rose knew how to live on a budget. She had a job as a teacher's aide at a local family center in her neighborhood. A job that she was good at and loved.

Her best friend Ashley worked there as well and the two usually walked to the center together. The center was just six blocks away from Roses' house. Rose sometimes didn't like to walk because of the numerous men that flirted with her and Ashley along the way. They were always besieged with unwanted advances from men driving, walking, riding bikes or just standing around.

"Well... hello beautiful," an elderly male neighbor watering his gas greeted. "Hi," Rose replied, a she dashed past him hoping not to miss her ride. Everyone in the neighborhood knew of Rose they just didn't know her personally. She was the quiet beauty who always seemed in a rush. Rose kept to herself and only spent time with Ashley and her grandmother Elouise.

"Wait!" Rose shouted, as the bus sat prepared to take off. "Sorry," she said, as she boarded.

"No problem," the driver said. Rose sat down and pulled her phone. She looked around. Her friend Ashley was even worse with punctuality. They would be late for their own funerals.

Rose decided to call Ashley and make sure she was on her way. Ashley overslept sometimes and would be late or just wouldn't bother to show up. *Damn! She's not answering,* Rose thought, as the bus stopped at another stop. It was too late. The next bus wouldn't be along until a half hour. But still Rose tried.

Their boss was lenient most times as long as they made an effort. Her job was not too far away. Another seven or eight blocks and she would be at the center. Too far to walk and close enough to make it on time if she was diligent. The bus slowed. Her stop was coming up. Rose smiled at the familiar face waiting. Ashley chewed gum and stared at her nails, as she waited on Rose.

"Girl, I just tried to call you. I thought you overslept," Rose said.

"I did. I had to hurry and get ready so that Jay could drop me off," Ashley replied.

Rose got quiet, looked straight and continued to walk with Ashley. That name did something to her. She didn't like Jay. He was Ashley's mother's boyfriend and was a violent and abusive drunk. Rose didn't understand how Ashley's mother still kept him around. It was no secret that he messed with girls. And his determination to get close to Rose made her a target.

Her youth and inexperience at the time made her vulnerable to the predator. And then one night, without warning, he struck. He assaulted Rose as Ashley slept nearby. Rose remembered hearing his footsteps as he crept into the basement. She pretended to be sleep hoping he would go away. Fear had her unable to stop trembling, and he pull the covers back.

Jay held his hand over her mouth and whispered threats in her ear. He forced himself on her, turning her over and sodomizing her, as Ashley slept just a few feet away. He told her he would hurt her if she told anyone. He warned her that no one would believe her. Rose internalized the attack. It was the most vicious of all the attacks she had suffered. Being in foster care was not without trauma.

She had her ways of coping. It was always *join them and eat,* or fight against the grain and starve. And when Jay threatened her, she believed him. She never told anyone. Her silence made her a bigger target. His comfort at getting away with it had him being bold as ever.

He stalked her for a while, showing up at her home at all times of the night. She was terrified of him. The assault was damaging to her already fragile spirit. It was a scar that would be added to all the other scars of her young life. Rose had always wondered if he ever hurt Ashley. She thought that if he could do something so violent to her, what else was he capable of.

*R*ose was a striking and voluptuous twenty-six year old with hazel green eyes, long wavy brown hair and smooth caramel skin. She oozed sex appeal and had a walk that commanded attention. Rose was sweet, shy and remarkably beautiful. She stood 5'6 tall, with a 25-inch waist and an ass that women envied. Not that these features did her any good.

She felt plagued by her beauty and blamed herself for some of the things she had endured. The night Jay attacked her was the last night that she stayed at Ashley's. The attack had brought back memories of a childhood marred with abuse and neglect. Rose tried to forget about Jay as she entered the classroom filled with happy children. Children she hoped were not smiling to cover pain. It was something she did. Play pretend in order to protect the devils that frightened her so. The center had a good program. These were inner city children from poor backgrounds. Some were foster kids. Rose had a special place in her heart for the unwanted people of society, especially children. And she loved the arts program. It allowed for the children to be creative. To forget their troubles. It was something positive. And helping them helped her heal through her own pain.

It was a long and tiring day. Rose was winding down after taking the kids on a field trip along with the teacher and other members of the staff. She had packed her bag and was walking towards the exit, when she was approached by Mr. Sullivan. The director of the center and one of her favorite people. He was consistent in his behavior. Just a nice, laid back man with a vision he believed was in the center's best interest.

"Hi Rose," Mr. Sullivan said.

"Hi Mr. Sullivan," Rose replied, as she slowed down so he could walk with her.

"There was a gentleman here earlier today. He's interested in recruiting young women to work with him part time, processing tax returns. He mentioned you and asked if I thought you would be interested in working with him. He works out of his home. He'd pay you in cash," he said.

"No thanks. I have a lot going on and I just don't have the time. Thanks. Tell him I thank him for the opportunity though," Rose replied, as she headed for the door.

"Ok. I'll be sure to let him know," he said, as he walked away.

Rose knew the man Mr. Sullivan was speaking of. He seemed obsessed with her and would go out of his way to speak. She was always uncomfortable with the way he looked at her. She was sure his invitation had an intention behind it. And she never trusted such offers. Rose avoided getting herself into situations where she would possibly be alone with a man she didn't know. Even though she struggled to make ends meet and needed the extra money, she wouldn't accept such offers from strangers. She had been the victim of assaults that seemed innocent upfront so she was cautious.

Rose jumped back on the bus and headed for home. She didn't see Ashley before she left and decided she would call her to catch up. She didn't want to be anywhere around if Jay was coming to pick her up from work. Rose looked out the window as she sat there consumed with thoughts. She spent a lot of time thinking about her past. She was a woman now, on her own and making her on way. But she struggled with the demons inside her head. *My stop!* Rose said as she jumped up. She exited the bus and slowly walked towards her house hungry and tired.

"Rosalee," a voice called out in the distance. Rose continued walking, refusing to look back. She knew that voice and didn't want to be bothered.

"Rosalee, I need to talk to you," the voice said. Only one person called her by that name, Tina Walker, her mother. Rose turned around and stopped long enough for Tina to catch up.

"Hey. I saw you walking. I was over there talking to Hank," Tina said.

"What do you want Tina? I'm tired. I just got off work," Rose replied.

"I just need a few dollars. I'll give it back to you. I need to catch a cab home. I don't stay on Wick St. anymore. I moved further south over near 106th," Tina said.

Rose reached in her pocket and handed Tina a five dollar bill. "That's all I can give you. I don't have anymore," Rose said, as she turned and continued toward her house.

"Thanks baby. I love you," Tina replied, as she walked off. Tina was well known in the neighborhood and hustled the streets sometimes as her daughter walked by.

*T*ina Walker was a stunning beauty herself at one time. It was in her genes, passed down from generations of beautiful women with all the bells and whistles, as if they were manufactured right off of an assembly line. But being constantly approached, flirted with and seduced with promises of riches was more than the beautiful Tina could handle.

She had given birth to Rose at the age of fourteen and ran the streets everyday with baby in tow. Rose was a beautiful child and people took notice. Tina enjoyed the attention but was a child herself and ill-prepared to take care of Rose. Social Services removed Rose from Tina's care several times citing child safety issues. Tina was uneducated, using drugs, hooking and dancing in strip clubs to get by. The placements never lasted long for the shy withdrawn Rose. There was always a problem with the wives who shunned the young girl or with their husbands who couldn't seem to keep their hands to themselves.

For most of the families, Rose was merely a paycheck. And with minimal resources and a drunk for a husband, her grandmother Elouise was in no position to take care of her. Being with Tina didn't help the situation for the young Rose. Tina didn't protect her daughter and was too busy doing adult things in her young teenage years to care. Rose had once been molested in Tina's care, right in Tina's face. Rose had been so viscously attacked that doctors said she wouldn't be able to have children of her own. Roses childhood experiences ultimately drove a wedge between her and her mother.

As Rose grew up and puberty began, her body started developing at a fast pace. With puberty came the constant unwelcomed advances from young men. By the age of thirteen, Rose had the figure of a young lady much older than her years. Boys and men took notice, and Rose found herself involved in many inappropriate situations. It wasn't until the age of fifteen, when Rose was permanently placed with her grandmother, that her trouble filled life began to have some stability. But that stability was short lived. Rose didn't like being around her grandfather Mr. Walker when he drank and so by nineteen, Rose was on her own.

She moved into a small modest two-bedroom rental in a very poor section of the city. The home was in poor condition but Rose didn't mind. The rent was affordable, the landlord was a woman and she was close to her grandmother's house. The woman's husband had only come by twice in the last year to collect the rent which was two times too many. On both occasions he propositioned Rose and told her that if she let him have his way, he would not collect any money from her. Rose was used to being propositioned in exchange for money or favors. But she didn't sell her body to men and would rather beg for it on the street. She despised the fact that her mother was a prostitute and such offers disgusted her.

***

It was going to be dark soon and Rose realized she had not eaten since breakfast. She had the weekend off and had planned to just relax. *I wonder what Ashley's doing? Maybe she's hungry too and we can go get a bite to eat before it gets too late. I better call her now*, she thought. Rose had no money to buy food and payday was a week away. She decided to call Ashley and see if she wanted to grab a bite to eat.

"Hey Girl what you doing?" Rose asked.

"Nothing really. On my mother's laptop. She's drunk as hell and passed out right now," Ashley remarked.

"Well, I was going to get something to eat. Want to come?" Rose asked.

"Yeah but I have no money," Ashley replied.

"Neither do I Ashley that never stopped us before. We'll get it. Maybe momma Elouise has some money. We'll stop by there on the way. We just need a few dollars," Rose suggested.

"Ok. I'll be there in a sec," she replied.

Rose and Ashley decided to make their way to the downtown area of Chicago where there would be lots of people. Rose liked downtown with its wonderful tall buildings and well-lit streets. The surroundings made Rose feel protected, because people were always coming and going. She didn't have to worry about being pulled into a dark alley or grabbed and forced into an abandoned house. She felt safe.

As they walked toward the bus stop, Ashley told Rose that she found money between the couch.

"It's just a few dollars. Enough to get on the bus," she said.

The women had walked just a few blocks before spotting Roses' mom Tina coming their way. "Do you see who's coming?" Ashley cautioned.

"What is she even doing over here? She lives on the other side of town now," Rose remarked.

"Rosalee Bella Walker. Where are you going?" Tina yelled out, as she approached them.

"Nowhere," Rose replied.

The three women stood there for what seemed like an eternity before Ashley chimed in to break the ice. "Hey Tina. Haven't seen you in a minute. You been ok?" she said.

"Yeah I'm good. Came to see how Rose is," Tina said, looking at Rose. "You know, you could at least call me. I worry about you" Tina said, as she pulled a pack of Camel cigarettes from her pocket.

"Yeah," Rose replied.

Rose had washed her hands of Tina years ago and felt uncomfortable in her presence.

"Where you going?" Tina repeated.

"To get something to eat," Rose answered, then looked away.

Her agitated mood was obvious to Tina and so she didn't force the issue. She had given up trying to win her daughter's approval. But she still made occasional attempts to be in her life. "You got money?" asked Tina.

"No, but we'll get some," replied Rose.

"How? Are you going to beg for it on the street? You should stop doing that Rose. It's not safe," Tina replied, as she lit her cigarette.

"I don't do that anymore. And don't talk to me about being safe," Rose fumed, as she began to walk away.

Tina reached in her pocket and pulled out twenty dollars. She extended her hand to Rose. She hoped Rose would take the money. She wanted to feel needed. It was always important to Tina to try and help Rose if she could. The guilt of being an absent mother weighed heavy on her at times. She wished they leaned on each other. She yearned for a more give and take relationship with her only child. Rose looked at the money then turned her head.

"I don't want that!" she said.

Tina shook her head and then handed the money to Ashley, "Make sure she gets something to eat," she said.

"Ok," replied Ashley.

Tina walked off toward her mother Elouise's house as Rose and Ashley continued down the street. Ashley was quiet. She could see that Roses' demeanor had completely changed. Tina had that effect on her. Rose was sweet, quiet and generous to a fault. But whenever Tina came around, Rose would respond with attitude and resentment.

"Why does she do that? Just show up. I wouldn't care if I never saw her again," Rose said.

"That's your mother Rose. She loves you the best way she knows how," Ashley replied, walking slow and looking around.

It was a pleasant afternoon and she hoped Tina's unwelcomed pop up visit, didn't put Rose in a bad mood. She loved her friend and she understood the dynamic of their relationship. She had a strained relationship with her mother as well, so she knew their struggles.

"I don't care Ash. You have no idea. Not a clue. She let men mess with me. She didn't care. I needed her and she wasn't there. Always high. Always passed out. She ruined my life. She can't make up for that now," Rose expressed.

The women had enough money for the bus with some left over to get something to eat. Roses' plan was to get something and then get home quickly so she could check on her grandmother Elouise. She lived just a few blocks from Rose and was the mother Tina never could be. Rose adored her grandmother..

***

A soft bell rang as they entered the diner. "We would like to order something to go," Ashley said to the waiter, who pointed in the direction of the cash register.

"Hi. Can we get two burgers and two orders of fries and a coke," Ashley said.

"Sure honey. No problem," the gentleman said, as he stared at Rose.

Rose remembered the older, handsome gentleman. He had offered her a position as a waitress at one time, but she turned him down. He had made numerous unwelcomed advances on a number of occasions and Roses' instincts warned her to stay away.

"Ok here you go. That'll be eleven dollars and fifty-three cents," he said.

Ashley handed the man twenty dollars to pay the bill then tried to give Rose the change.

"I don't want her money Ashley. I don't need anything from her now. It's too late! I won't be bought! She can't buy me after everything she has done," Rose said.

Ashley shook her head in disbelief then pocketed the change. It was of no use to argue. Rose was stubborn. And she understood her friends' pain. She too had a mother that made the worst of choices. They were friends who had the same types of suffering. Sexual abuse by men they were supposed to trust. Ashley bumped Rose then chuckled. She hoped to get her out of the mood she was in. Tina could turn sun into rain. But they were good. They had food. They had their grandmother's and they both had each other. The sun would shine again.

The women took the next bus and headed back towards their neighborhood. Rose stared out the window at the dilapidated homes. The plight was hard to watch. She wanted out but it didn't seem in the cards for her. Rose sighed. This was her life. She was making the best of it. Money would always be an issue. She was learning how to make a dollar stretch. She wondered how she was going to make it through the next few days with the few dollars she had.

Maybe I'll borrow some from nanna, she thought, hoping Elouise had received her check in the mail. Her grandmother was her touchstone. A woman of faith who was never disloyal or hurtful. Elouise would give her whatever she asked for but she tried not to abuse her generosity. She had needs too and was living on a fixed income. *I'll just borrow forty. That will be enough*, Rose thought.

"I'll call you tomorrow," Rose said, as the two women walked off the bus and towards their neighborhood.

"Make sure you call me. I met this guy. Gurllll…He is all that. We supposed to go out," Ashley said. Rose's eyes popped.

"Oh really. You tell me that *now* that I have to go," Rose joked.

"Yeah girl. I didn't want to say anything until I saw he was serious. Besides…Marco been calling back again. I think I should just be single for now. You know how I get. Wishy washy as hell," Ashley said.

Rose laughed. Ashley described herself brilliantly. She was quick to change her mind. She feared getting close to men. But not nearly in the way Rose did. Rose was avoiding men completely even though she had dreams of being in love. It would take someone special. Otherwise, she was going it as a single woman.

Rose watched as Ashley headed towards her home. The two had known each other since childhood. They grew up in the same neighborhood and attended some of the same schools. Their friendship had gone through a rough patch and they didn't speak for years after. It was an incident they hadn't brought up since. It was still too touchy of a subject and Rose still thought of it. The pain was still there.

Rose walked and glanced back. Her mind went to the incident. It was another one of her issues. Her inability to forget things. Her trauma stirred beneath the surface always rising and making a fresh cut in her flesh. It was innocent enough. She was sexually involved with one of Ashley's brother's and ended up involved with a second brother as well. They seemed to be taking turns flirting. Liquor only added to the absence of better judgement. They had all been drinking and partying when things went too far. Rose ended up sleeping with one then the other. It all seemed a big blur and she blamed the alcohol, although she seemed more than intoxicated. Soon, Rose made claims that it was not consensual and her and Ashley's friendship suffered the consequences. It took years to patch up their broken sisterhood. In the end, Ashley ended up siding with Rose. And the two made amends.

"Who is it?" replied Elouise.

"It's me ma," Rose yelled through the door.

Rose was close to her grandmother, who was instrumental in raising her. Rose referred to her grandmother as her mother and Tina was simply "Tina".

"Hi baby. Come on in. Are you staying?" her grandmother Elouise said.

"Yeah. Tina come by here?" Rose asked.

"She was here for a minute then she left. She said she'd be back tomorrow," replied Elouise, as she walked back into her living room.

"You want some fries?" Rose asked, as she sat down and opened her bag of food.

"No baby. I just ate. You been ok? I haven't seen you in a few days. I was starting to worry," Elouise said, in a concerned voice. Rose stayed just a few blocks away and Elouise was used to her stopping by more often.

She worried about Rose more than she worried about her own daughter Tina. Grandma Elouise knew Tina was capable of handling herself, but she wasn't so sure about Rose.

"I've been okay. I'm working with some new children down at the center," she said. "I'm pretty tired. I'm going to go lay down for a minute before I head home," Rose said, as she went to the spare bedroom that was once her room.

Rose planned on getting a quick nap in, then leaving. She was aware that her grandmother's house, albeit comfortable and relaxing, could flip into something unpleasant. Tina had a habit of showing up drunk or high and was always making a scene. Rose avoided going to Tina's house because there was always some man over and that man always wanted a piece of Rose. Tina never managed to stay with the same man for more than a few short months before there would be some new creepy guy hanging around.

Her taste is men was completely based on self-gratification. Whoever could pay and keep the drugs flowing won the prize. Tina had tried several times in the past to trade her daughter for sex in exchange for drugs or money. But Rose usually managed to get away. The more Tina drank and used drugs, the more likely she was to try and sell her daughter.

Tina could be aggressive when coming down off of a drug high or drinking binge and Rose didn't like to be around for the fallout. Her grandmother had given up trying to actually win battles with Tina, but there would still be war. Elouise had some fight left in her at her old age and she resented Tina's attempts to use her daughter to feed her drug habit. Roses' plan was to get some rest and leave before dawn. She didn't want Tina showing up with one of her gentleman friends and getting any ideas.

Tina had lost her youthful good looks years before. She used every opportunity to try to get Rose to engage in sexual encounters with her male companions. She figured she could get more out of them if they were given access to her beautiful daughter. To her, Rose was sitting on a meal ticket. She believed it was a waste to have beauty and a body and not use it for financial gain.

But Rose was never interested in that. She hoped to find true love one day. Not money and gifts in exchange for lust. Rose avoided such men. Rose was skilled at downplaying her looks and physique in an attempt to go unnoticed. She shunned the attention of men because men had been a source of pain in her life. And since she couldn't trust them, she decided to avoid them altogether.

Rose always blamed her looks and voluptuous physique for drawing the unwanted attention, and over time, put increasing effort into downplaying her physical attributes. As she got older, she became strongly attracted to men but feared getting into a serious relationship because of her past. It had been awhile since she had dated anyone, despite the many opportunities. No one stood a chance with the cautious and reluctant Rose. She had given up on meeting anyone special, that is, until a dashing young gentleman by the name of Max Stone walked into her life.

Chapter Two – Max

Max was a handsome man, athletically built, with chiseled cheek bones and a sharp jawline. His sexy, almond shaped brown eyes left women imagining some of the most erotic and kinky thoughts about him. There was no shortage of female interest, but Max was a man who liked to keep his options open.

He had his share of one-night stands and heated sexual tryst in the local bar restrooms. He had experienced things other men jot down on their bucket list. Multiple partners at one time. Receiving fellatio in the back of his Escalade. Giving head to his father's secretary in his father's office. All were mere drops in the bucket of the life of Maximillian Ulysses Stone.

Max's sexual prowess was enviable. He had a long line of women hoping to get a chance with the skilled lover. He could have his way with just about any women he wanted, but Max preferred blondes. He would date women with absolutely no ambition or drive, as long as they were gorgeous.

This fact didn't sit to well with his father. He showed his disapproval by constantly setting Max up on dates with beautiful, successful women. Max showed his contempt for his father's meddling by fucking the women and leaving them heartbroken and full of revenge.

Max was an only child and his father worked hard to get him aligned with the family business. He had put in long hours building their business and he wasn't going to watch Max destroy it. His father had to pay off several despondent women. Women who were complaining of sexual misconduct and dragging the Stone name through the mud.

As a peace offering to his father, Max promised to look for and marry, a successful woman. He also promised to produce heirs that would make his father proud. His father showed his appreciation by promoting his son which meant a high, six figure salary. Deep down, Max resented his father's attempts at controlling him. *The nerve of him. In my business about who I'm fucking when he's constantly fucking around on my mother*, Max thought.

It was rumored that Max Sr. had fathered a few children while still married to Max's mom. His father had fucked women young enough to be his daughter and managed to fuck every secretary that walked through the doors of *Max Stone Law Firm.* Max had even walked in on his father, naked from the waist down, performing cunnilingus on a client's wife. A major scandal since the client was in a meeting with another attorney down the hall.

Max was holding on to a *pinch sized* amount of respect for his father. His mother didn't know of her husband's conquest and that was all that concerned Max. His mother was important to him, and as long as she was happy, he could deal with whatever his father was talking about.

Max's personal life was a series of one-night stands with hidden agendas when he first met Rose. He was at the family center for an appointment, when he spotted Rose walking down the hall. He stopped and smiled at her as she was about to enter one of the classrooms. Rose immediately noticed Max. He was too handsome to ignore. Until the moment she'd met him, other men she ran across just kind of blended into the abyss. Into an endless sea of uninteresting men. But not Max. He stood out.

With his model good looks and strong street style presence, Rose quickly became smitten. Max stood 5'11 inches tall, with smooth caramel colored skin and natural hair. His hair was long and he liked to wear it neat and loose. His striking features made him look more like a male model than an attorney. He was an up and coming attorney, from a prominent family, and had access to the deep pockets of his father. Max was self-assured, sophisticated, and charming.

Business suits were his preferred attire and his suits were tailored made to fit him like a glove. He preferred a more fitted style and his taste was impeccable. His father provided well for his family and he had high expectations of his son. Max entertaining random women and going "slumming" with the local pretty girl down at the center, was not one of them. But Max was beyond smitten and wasted no time making his introduction.

"Hi. My name is Max, beautiful. How's your day?" he said. He had a million-dollar smile that exposed teeth so perfect, they appeared to be a row of chiclets.

"Good, nice to meet you. I'm Rose," she said. "Are you here with your family?" she asked.

"No," replied Max. "I'm here on business. I'm meeting with Mr. Sullivan and his team to discuss future projects and to make a donation in the name of my families' law firm," he replied.

"You're a lawyer?" Rose asked.

"Yeah. Unfortunately. What about you?" he asked, still grinning as he stood enchanted by her beauty.

"I teach art to the children here at the center," she replied, blushing from his undeterred stare.

"Oh. Well can you get away sometime? I would love to take you out," Max asked.

"I'm pretty busy. I'm not sure when I would be able to get away," she replied.

She wanted to trust the moment and go with it, but her fears began to set in. Rose was not sure she actually wanted to go on a date with Max. After all, she had just met him. *What if he's crazy? What if he tries to take advantage of me on the date?*

Roses' mind raced, as she contemplated what to say. But after a moment of doubt, she relaxed a bit. She took a deep breath and then agreed to go out on a date with him.

Max smiled. He really wanted to take her out and for a minute, he wasn't sure she would say yes. "What about tomorrow? Where should I pick you up from?" he asked.

The question sent Roses' mind racing again. She didn't want him to see where she lived. "Can you meet me here? I'll be here in the morning. I'm usually done around two o'clock," she said.

"Great, I'll see you then beautiful," Max said, as he walked toward the main office for his meeting.

He glanced back a few times until he made his way through the door. He couldn't take his eyes off of her. He sensed the hesitation in her voice when he asked to take her out. He wasn't quite sure what to make of it. He shrugged it off and entered the main office for his meeting with Mr. Sullivan. Max knew he'd see her Friday and he figured that her hesitation stemmed from first date jitters, nothing more.

Rose walked toward the class where she helped the children with their art projects. She was nervous but excited about the date she had just made with the handsome gentleman. Rose couldn't remember when a man so intrigued her. Maybe he was the one. The one her grandmother always told her about. Grandma Elouise always told Rose that her other half was out there in the world and that one day he would find her. Her grandma was old school in her beliefs. She had profound feelings about the institution of marriage and the importance of family.

Elouise married young and stayed with Mr. Walker until his death from alcohol abuse at the age of fifty-six. Rose had faith in what her grandmother told her. She wanted to believe in it. After all, she believed in love and wanted to have a family of her own someday despite the trials of her younger life. She had a strong desire to bond and connect with members of the opposite sex. Her sexual desires were strong and she longed to be intimate with the right man. Rose had moments of promiscuity as a young teenager but had become less sexually active with men as she got older. Her desires were still strong but she opted for self-gratification versus intimacy with men.

She had a high libido that bordered on nymphomania and she desired orgasms frequently. She had resorted to playing with herself and had become quite skilled at bringing herself to multiple orgasms effortlessly. She loved self-pleasure and eventually began to prefer it over intercourse with a man. Rose had not been intimate with a man in some time. She wanted something serious and felt she was ready. *Is*

Max the man of my dreams? The man who sweeps me off my feet and we live happily ever after? she wondered.

***

Friday morning was a good morning for Rose. She made a visit to grandma Elouises' for breakfast and a warm shower. She hated showers at her place. The landlord was slow at repairs and the plumbing in the bathroom was not working properly. The shower water trickled out and was never warm enough. But all those issues didn't deter Rose and she looked forward to her date. Rose was beaming from thoughts of a first date with Max.

"Hi baby, you look so happy today. You having a good morning so far?" Elouise said, as she sat in her recliner watching her favorite morning programs.

"I feel good today ma. Today's going to be a good day. I met a guy," Rose said, as she walked toward the bathroom to freshen up before her date.

"You did? Who is he? Do I get to meet him?" replied Elouise, excited that her granddaughter was going on a date.

Elouise thought Rose didn't get out much and she wanted her granddaughter to experience more of what life had to offer. "Yes! Eventually! Let me get to know him. See what he's about first. Then I'll introduce you," Rose said, in her usual soft voice.

"Ok. But I want to know where you're going. Just in case," Elouise replied.

"Just in case what ma? He's not a serial killer. I'll be fine. They know him at the shelter. He's a lawyer," Rose stated, as she fixed her hair.

"Well ok baby. If you say so. But still call me and let me know you're ok," replied Elouise.

"Ok ma," Rose said, as she grabbed her purse. She kissed Elouise and told her she would see her later as she rushed out the door.

Rose made it to the center early. She continued her tasks with the children and made sure to wrap things up timely so she wouldn't be running late when Max arrived. As she prepared for the final assignments, her friend Ashley walked in. "Rose, who is that fine ass man that just walked in asking for you?" she said. Rose smiled and continued helping one of the children draw a house. "That's Max. I met him the other day." "Max! You Haven't told me about no Max girl. Damn! Who is he?" replied Ashley.

Rose was shy and reluctant to speak about her personal affairs, even with someone as close to her as Ashley. Ashley was the one and only friend. The friend with similar experiences. The friend who snuck her in the basement to sleep undetected from her drunk and belligerent mother. But Rose had a need for privacy and always needed time to open up and talk.

"I'll tell you about him later. I'll call you when I get home. Right now, I have to go. Can you put the rest of these projects away for me?" asked Rose.

"Sure," replied Ashley. "I'm not playing Rose. You better call me later so we can talk," Ashley said, looking intensely at her.

"Ok," Rose said, as she made her way towards the door.

As Rose walked toward the exit, she could see Max standing there with his hands in his pockets and a big smile on his face. "Hi beautiful. You ready?" he said. "Yeah I'm ready," replied Rose. "Where you want to go first?" asked Max. "First?" Rose replied. "Yeah. You pick the restaurant and then I'm going to take you to a special place afterwards. A surprise. You'll like it. You'll have fun. Trust me," he said. Rose began to get nervous. The words "trust" and "men" weren't synonymous where she came from. But there was something about Max's calm demeanor and warm smile that made Rose comfortable for the first time in her life and it felt right.

***

Max tried to see Rose every day for the next several weeks. He cancelled appointments and worked less hours in an attempt to see her as often as he could. He wondered why Rose had not invited him to her home. She was having him pick her up from her grandmother's or Ashely's house. "Why can't I come to your house? Do you live with someone? You got a man?" Max asked, as they walked holding hands. "I assumed you probably had a man. You're too pretty to be single," he said, hoping he was wrong. He was head over heels in love with her. They had spent every day, for the last couple of months, together. "No Max. That's not it at all," Rose replied, as she paused and looked around. "One day you will."

The next day, Rose prepared for an evening with Max. He told her he would pick her up from Elouises' home after he left his appointment. She was excited and couldn't wait to see him. Max was fun and she liked how playful he was with her. She walked through her house cleaning up in an attempt to make her modest home look nice. She was ready to invite him over. She felt close to him and she was ready to open up and share more of her life with him.

Rose walked through her kitchen and could hear her phone ringing in the distance. She ran to her bedroom and grabbed her cell phone. "Hello," she answered. "Hey girl. What are you up to?" Ashley asked. "Oh. Hey. Just cleaning up in case I invite Max over after dinner tonight," Rose replied. "Oh. I see things are still going good between you two. You're with him every day Rose. That's good. That means he's in love," Ashley replied. Rose paused before continuing. She had something serious to talk about.

"Max asked me to move in with him," she said, as she sat down on her bed. "What! Really! Already," Ashley said, surprised but not completely shocked by the news. Max was spending every moment possible with her friend and so she knew that he would press forward onto something more serious. "Wow Rose. That's fast. You just met him. But he seems like a good man and he is definitely in love with you," she said. "I know. I feel like I've known him forever. I see him just about every day. And I'm in love with him too. It's just all so sudden," Rose replied.

"Have you met his family?" Ashley asked. "No, not yet. He's an only child. He's from a small family like I am," Rose said. "Has he met Tina or momma Elouise?" Ashley asked. "No! He'll never meet Tina. You know I'm not going to let him meet her. He met nanna though. I don't know Ash. Well, I better get going. He'll be on his way in a few hours. I have to walk around to nanna's house. I'll call you tomorrow," she said. Rose hung up the phone and just stared off into space.

She began to think of a life with Max. She wondered what he would think if he knew about the details of her life. She didn't want Max to know about her childhood and about her mother Tina.

His mother is an educated woman. His father is a lawyer. He's a lawyer! What would he think if he knew my mother was a prostitute. A high school dropout. What if he knew about me, she thought.

Rose and Max were caught up in a whirlwind romance and Max had asked her to move in after just ten weeks of dating. Rose was worried and she had a lot to think about. But she had fallen in love with him and wanted to move on with her life. Rose decided at that moment, that she would trust her instincts and take a chance. She loved him.

*I*t was a beautiful morning and Rose was at home relaxing while Max was away on business. Home was a downtown Chicago high-rise condominium, a far cry from the humble life she'd left behind. A life she didn't miss, as she quickly became accustomed to her lavish surroundings. She still made time to see momma Elouise and her girlfriend Ashley. But Rose had not seen her mother Tina in months. Rose contemplated what to do for the day as she made her way to the kitchen to make a cup of coffee.

She loved the smell of coffee. It reminded her of her first date with Max. Their romantic walks through Hines Park, surrounded by beautiful flowers and picturesque landscaping. The park where she had her first kiss with Max. The park where she first made love to Max. Rose liked to relive some of those first few dates with Max. Those wonderful moments of discovery and anticipation.

As she slowly sipped her coffee, she couldn't help but reminisce on the past few months. How it had started out slow and quickly grew into the best thing in her life or so it seemed. Max was a romantic and was in love with Rose. The only problem was that sexually, Max was alone in this romance.

Rose thought of Max and how she'd felt after their lovemaking sessions. Max seemed inadequate to Rose. She had not had a single orgasm with him, not one. She had resorted to masturbating when Max wasn't around. As spontaneous and kinky as Max could be, he was unable to bring Rose to orgasm. And why not? she wondered. He loved to eat pussy. He would do it for long periods of time moaning and groaning as if he were on the receiving end. The size of his male part was more than enough to satisfy any woman. Slightly larger than average and capable of intense, long-standing erections.

Max liked to fuck and he liked to fuck everywhere. He was an adventurous lover, pulling over to the side of the road to engage in various sexual acts. Max preferred the outdoors. He shared his fantasies with Rose, who had become quite comfortable in her own skin. She was opening up and was beginning to explore her own sexual needs. Max's enthusiasm and desire to please Rose left her confused as to why she wasn't able to come with him.

Is it me? Have I been playing with myself for so long that my vagina prefers only me? Am I holding back because of my past? I thought I was over all of that, maybe not, she thought.

Roses' confusion was compounded by the fact that when she touched herself, she would have an orgasm within minutes. Her orgasms were intense, sending ripples of waves through her abdomen and making its way up her body. Rose had never experienced such intense orgasms with a man. Some of the few short-lived romances she'd had before, were similar to what she was experiencing with Max.

But Rose was older now, and she believed that a man was capable of giving her an orgasm. And she hoped that it would be Max. *Maybe if he takes his time and include more foreplay, I will be able to come.* Rose thought. Max liked foreplay but could never hold out long enough when it came to Rose. He was always anxious to be inside her. Like being cuddled up in a warm blanket.

I need to tell him I want more foreplay without breaking the news to him that I have never had an orgasm, Rose thought. She shook her head. It didn't seem that complicated. He excited her. Just not in the bedroom. *That's it. Maybe if we try more foreplay* she thought. She was willing to try anything. She didn't want to lose him.

"Baby! I'm back," shouted Max, as he walked through the door of his luxury condo. Rose had just taken a shower and ran to him, robe open, and embraced him with open arms and a passionate kiss. "Hi baby I missed you," replied Rose. "I need you now baby. I can't wait. I thought about this ass all day," Max said, as he whisked Rose to their bedroom. It wasn't hard to get in the mood in their bedroom. Candles throughout, white plush carpet with white and grey custom-made furniture. There were mirrors everywhere and the room was a picture-perfect setting of romantic ambience.

Max picked Rose up as she wrapped her legs around his waist. He laid her down on the bed then stared at her and gave her sexy looks as he undressed. He loved to watch her eyes as she watched him undress. Max had always enjoyed making women wait for it. He liked the look of anticipation on Roses' face while she watched him undress.

He slowly took his clothes off revealing his perfectly toned body and large penis. His penis was perfectly shaped, like a beautiful, tall mushroom designed specifically to enter into a women's vagina. Max had a weakness for head and wished Rose would indulge him more. But Rose was not to fond of head and had only performed it on Max a few times. Max didn't seem to mind, he enjoyed being inside of Rose.

As he began to kiss Rose's neck, slowly working his way down to her breast, Rose decided this was the moment. It was perfect timing for her to tell Max that she wanted him to spend more time kissing her body. That she wanted him to use his hands more and spend more time on their foreplay. "Max?" Rose said softly, as she moaned from his wet and tender kisses on her body. "Yes baby," Max replied, as he slowly kissed her breast and stomach.

"I want more foreplay. I want us to spend more time kissing and caressing one another," she said.

"Don't I always do that," Max replied, as he continued kissing her.

"Well. Not always," she replied.

Max paused and then resumed kissing Rose. "What do you mean? I'll take my time baby I just want you so bad sometimes," Max said, as he slowly kissed Roses' breast. Max worked his way down her body, kissing tenderly and planting warm kisses on her skin. He kissed on Rose and she moaned in ecstasy and he took his time sucking and kissing her pussy.

Rose thought that maybe he would be able to make her come this time. He was spending more time down there. He was kissing her more. He did everything longer, and then he entered her slowly. Max fucked Rose slow and deliberate for nearly a half an hour. He began to slow his pumping then stopped altogether and began kissing on her, a technique he often did to stop his ejaculation from coming too soon. Once he was ready, he entered Rose again and for another twenty-five minutes fucked her until he came.

His stamina was unbelievable. He had the energy of a gang of men. Max yelled out as he came hard in the throes of ecstasy. He lay on Rose with his penis still inside of her and fell asleep. She lay there frustrated because she still did not come. Her excitement had now turned to pure frustration. Max was oblivious to her not having an orgasm. Her moans led him to believe that she was having them. Max was completely unaware of Roses' frustration.

It's never going to happen, she thought. *He did everything I asked. Unbelievable. It's got be me. This is not on him. This is me. I have ruined my pussy forever,* she naively thought. *That's it, I guess. I better just get used to this because this is what it is!*

***

It's was 5:00 am on a brisk Friday morning when Max arose to start his day. He had a meeting scheduled at the office with his father. Stone Law Firm had an influx of clients and they needed to go over some of the corporate accounts he was handling. As Rose lay there sleeping, Max could not help but stare at her before he took his shower. He wanted to kiss her, but he knew she needed her rest.

They had been up all night making love and he figured she had to be tired. But Max couldn't help himself. With her beautiful wavy hair tousled across her face and the sheets covering only half of her well-toned body, Max wanted her again. *No, I better get in the shower. I'll be late,* he thought. He jumped in the shower, dressed and quickly sped off in his brand new custom burgundy convertible Chevy Camaro.

"Hi Sherilyn," Max said, as he entered the firm. "Oh, hi Max. Your father is waiting for you in conference room A," replied Sherilyn, smiling as Max walked past her. Sherilyn was new to the firm and Max had already had his way with her in the back of his Escalade in the office parking structure.

"Hi pop," Max said to his father, as he entered the conference room.

"Hey son come sit down. I got a new account I want to go over with you," his father said.

Max Stone Sr. was an accomplished attorney in his late sixties and he wanted to slow down on the accounts he personally handled. He planned on retiring soon and wanted his son prepared to handle the larger accounts. The account was that of a huge technologies firm called *Rockwater Technologies Corporation.*

"This account is very special. It was difficult to land, but I finally got a meeting with the owner. I got them to change firms and let us handle all their legal needs," said Max Sr. "The company has nineteen employees and is owned by a wealthy young gentleman named Boston St. Rock. He runs it along with his brothers. I think you'll like them. They are a very down to earth family," Max Sr. said, as he showed Max the file.

"Rockwater Technologies is on the cutting edge of technology and need help with patents and reviews of upcoming deals. The company also receives lots of lawsuits. They are always faced with lawsuits. Lawsuits from competitors but mostly from women. Women who make claims of sexual harassment after they've been terminated. The brothers are quite popular with the ladies and so needless to say, there's always trouble brewing," he continued.

"Ok pop. I'll look over the file and if I have any questions or concerns, I'll let you know." Max walked away with the huge box filled with documents regarding some of *Rockwater's* past issues and their current legal needs. Before he reached the door, Max Sr. called his name. Max turned around. He knew his father well. His father always had something else to say and it was always about Max's personal life. "So, when am I going to meet your girlfriend? She's living with you now, right? Don't you think I should be meeting her soon?" he said. "Sure pop. Soon!" Max replied, as he turned and walked out.

Max was in no rush for his father to meet Rose. She was beautiful. She was eye candy. Rose turned heads wherever she went. But Max knew his father could care less. Max Sr. would be disappointed if he found out that Max's new girlfriend was an uneducated, penniless woman with no impressive background to talk about. Max Sr. talked down about such women. He expected Max to get involved with and marry someone from one of the wealthy and well-known families that they associated with.

Max entered his office, placed the box on his desk and sat at his computer. He needed to review his schedule for the day. He was hoping he had an opening that would allow him to shoot home for an early afternoon romp with Rose. He was still thinking of her and wanted to be with her again.

Max was insatiable when it came to Rose. He looked at his phone as he waited for his computer to turn on. He hoped Rose was up. If she was, then maybe she had tried to call him. Rose kept up with Max and the two talked constantly, even when he was at work. He was always taking time to talk to her and even engage in phone sex with her. Anything to stay connected to the love of his life.

"Damn," he said, as he looked at his itinerary. Max realized he had a full day of appointments lined up. Max picked up the phone and called the front desk. "Sherilyn," he said angrily. "Yes," she replied. "Why do you have my whole day filled? I asked you several times not to do that," Max said. "I'm sorry. There was no one else to take those appointments and those are the larger clients," she said. "Your father told me to give those appointments to you," replied Sherilyn. Max hung up in frustration. He knew that

Sherilyn did that in order to keep him at the office. She was in love with Max and he believed, she was aware of his afternoon quickies with his live-in girlfriend.

Rose awoke, slowly rolling over and stretching her body. Her and Max had made love all through the night and she had only gotten a few hours of sleep. She loved Max and the thought of leaving him over sex seemed ridiculous to her. *Maybe I should see someone. A doctor or perhaps a specialist,* Rose thought, as her hands slowly moved down towards her vagina. She needed to masturbate. She wanted to have the orgasm she felt cheated out of. It wasn't fair that Max had come, several times even, and she had not reached her own sexual gratification.

Rose slowly rubbed her clit and used her fingers to go inside with increasing momentum and pressure. She had a technique in which she rubbed her clitoris between her index and middle fingers using Vaseline and pressed lightly together while moving up and down. The sensation increased and Rose moaned in ecstasy as she came in her hand. It was a hard and intense orgasm that left her tired yet completely fulfilled. Rose lay there for a few minutes while she pulled herself together. She was tired and drained but she wanted to start her day. She was going to visit Elouise. She wanted to go early and take her some groceries and pick up her medicine.

Roses' phone began to vibrate. *Oh, it's Max. I know what he wants. No afternoon quickie today,* she thought.

"Hello?" Rose said.

"What you doing baby? I miss you. I want to come home and see you right quick before I take my first appointment," Max said.

"Not now Max. I'm going to see momma today," replied Rose.

"Can she wait baby? What's the rush? Come on. I need you," Max said, in an eager voice.

"No Max she can't. I have to go soon. She needs food and she'll need her medicine," replied Rose.

"You want me to take you," Max replied.

"No. I'm going to go now, so I can get back and start dinner. I won't be gone long, ok?" Rose said, in a concerned voice. She didn't want to hurt Max's feelings. She did love him. Rose always tried to keep Max happy and content, despite her own frustrations with their relationship.

"Ok baby I'll see you tonight," Max said, as he hung up the phone.

*R*ose made a run to the market and then to the pharmacy. She grabbed groceries and Elouise's medicine and then headed to her house. She pulled up and walked to the door then began to knock. She knocked several times as she looked around at her old neighborhood. "Ma," she yelled out, as she stood there knocking. After a few minutes she walked to the back door and knocked again. *Why is she taking so long?* she thought, as she waited. After a few minutes, Elouise opened the door. "Hi baby," Elouise said, happy to see her granddaughter. "Ma, what took you so long?" asked Rose. "I've been moving like a snail these days. I've got terrible aches and pains in my legs," Elouise said, as she slowly walked back into her living room.

"Well, I got your medicine. Maybe that'll help," Rose said, as she handed Elouise the bag. Rose walked into the kitchen to put away the groceries, wondering why Elouise was in so much pain. "Why have you been sitting here in pain?" Rose asked. "Well Tina came by and the next thing I knew I couldn't find any of my pain pills," Elouise admitted. "That's because she took them," Rose said, in anger. Rose continued putting away the groceries as she fumed. Tina had come and taken Elouises' medicine again. Tina loved her mother but would take advantage of her and go in her medicine. She would take most of what Elouise had, leaving one or two pills behind. Rose loved her mother but couldn't tolerate her drug use, which made her sneaky and unpredictable. *Damn shame,* Rose said, as she opened the refrigerator and placed the milk and sour cream inside.

Elouise and Rose continued putting the groceries away as they talked. Elouise wanted to play catch up with her granddaughter and wanted to know how things were going with Max. "So, how's it going with you and Max?" Elouise asked. "I guess everything's ok," replied Rose. "You guess ok? What kind of response is that?" replied Elouise. "Well ma, I don't know. I mean... He's a good guy. He treats me great. I have no issues there," Rose said. "Well then where are the issues?" asked Elouise. "I don't know," Rose replied.

"Rose! What do you mean you don't know? Is it sexual?" asked Elouise. Rose hesitated, she wanted to tell her nanna but she wasn't sure if she was ready to talk about it. She paused and then looked at Elouise. "Yes ma. I can't seem to have an orgasm with him and I don't know why. He's good in bed. Does everything a woman would desire. But somethings wrong. Wrong with me maybe," Rose said.

Elouise shook her head then smiled as if she had the answer. "I know what's wrong and it isn't with you," Elouise said, as she took her time talking. "He's not your other half," she continued, glancing up at Rose. They'd had this talk before. Elouise hoped that her talks with Rose had made a difference. She wanted what was best for her and she wanted her to be happy. She had told Rose, when she was a teenager, that there was a man in this world who was her soulmate. That when she grew up and started seriously dating, if she was lucky, she'd find him.

Rose stared at her grandmother. Elouise had said something she hadn't thought of. All this time she had been thinking that it was her when maybe, it was just good, old-fashioned chemistry. "But wait. I love him. I find him attractive. I thought that's what chemistry was. Oh my, I'm so confused right now," Rose said. "He's not the one Rose. That's all," Elouise said. "If he's not the one, then at some point you're going to have to end it. Otherwise, it will burn out like a flame and that's not fair to him," Elouise cautioned.

Rose stared at the wall. She was still confused. She loved Max. He made her laugh. He excited her. She longed for him. She missed him when he was away. Elouise was wrong. She loved her grandmother but she was wrong about this. She didn't know Max. She hadn't seen them together for long periods and she wasn't aware of the tight bond between them. Rose stood there as Elouise started making her lunch and came to a swift conclusion. *No, that's not it. He is the one! We're just at a snag in our relationship. Things will get better. I love him!*

Chapter Three – Boston

*H*eaded across town, Boston was running late, something he rarely did. Punctuality was important to him. He was hard-working, dedicated and brilliant. He had to be. He had a large family counting on him and his every move. His moves were precise, calculated and always lucrative. Boston was from a middle-class family. His father Orlando had managed to work and go to school at the same time, while raising a large family. Orlando finished with a master's degree and eventually landed a good paying job.

Orlando had moved the family out of the projects and into a middle-class neighborhood by the time his fifth born son Boston Augusta St. Rock arrived. Boston was a child prodigy and was tested for placement in a school for the gifted. But Boston refused to go to a private school. He didn't want to be away from his family and so he was allowed to remain in the Chicago Public School system.

Boston excelled with ease. By the time he graduated, he had two inventions patented and was working on a third. A high-tech device that could be attached to cell phones to remove viruses. Boston was a genius. His inventions made millions and by the time he was twenty-five, he was head of his own technologies company.

He proudly named the company after his families' surname St. Rock. *Rockwater Technologies* was a multi-million dollar company that specialized in creating technical devices and was ahead of its time. Boston and his brothers were developing things constantly and would sell their ideas to major brands for huge profits.

Boston was as handsome as he was smart. He was always well manicured and dressed in the finest clothes money could buy. He had the most flawless skin and kept himself in shape by working out at the gym and jogging. His clothes fit his physique perfectly as each suit was tailored to his strict guidelines. His tailor had to custom order every fabric from Italy and then meticulously go through them one by one checking quality, fabric content and the *feel* of the fabric.

Money was not an issue for Boston. He had been a multi-millionaire since he was twenty-five years old. Now at thirty-three, he had the world at his fingertips. He was wealthy enough to buy whatever he desired. He collected luxury watches, luxury cars and owned expensive homes in several major cities across the US. Boston was worldly and loved to travel. But as his company continued to grow, so did his responsibilities. His busy schedule meant no time for a social life. He had no time for chasing women or even falling in love. But women loved the St. Rock brothers, and Boston was at the top of the list.

The St. Rock's brothers looked like an assortment of Godiva chocolates, and Boston was the epitome of dark chocolate goodness. With his smooth skin, large almond eyes and a well-manicured mustache and goatee, his presence was just too powerful to ignore. He attracted women in droves. He and his brothers had their pick of the ladies since they were young teenagers dating. Their father had his hands full, keeping his sons in line. He had to keep constant watch over their dating lives. Orlando's main job was to keep his son's out of trouble and keep them from becoming fathers at an early age.

Boston was from a large family and it was a daunting task for his father. Orlando had ten boys and three girls to raise and he was determined that each one would reach their full potential. Their mother Cicely was a housewife. She did not interfere with her husbands' decisions on how their kids should be raised.

The one decision Orlando did not make was what the children's names would be. He left that up to Cicely. She decided that since she was a big fan of traveling, that she would name her children after major U.S. cities. The boys were named; Chicago, Bronx, Austin, Denver, Boston, Phoenix, Memphis, Columbus, Dallas and Dayton. She decided on the names; Aurora, Tacoma and Raleigh for the girls. Orlando was strict but fair and pushed his children to succeed academically. But Boston stood out and his father pushed him even harder because he saw a potential in him that needed to be nurtured and guided.

Boston arrived at his office, relaxed and ready to take his first meeting. "Mr. St. Rock, your first appointment is in a half hour with your lawyer Max Stone," his secretary said, as she handed him papers for his meeting. As Boston walked through the office, he stopped to speak with his brother Denver about the status of a project he was working on.

"Hey Den, how's that project going? You making any progress? I can help if you need me to," Boston said to his older brother.

"No, I just need to tweak the fine points on what the device will deliver and we're good," replied Denver.

Boston continued to his office so he could go over what he wanted to cover with his new lawyer Max. Boston had not met the younger Max Stone. He'd only met Max Stone Sr. who had informed him that all meetings would be handled by his son moving forward. And that he would only interject if a situation arose. "Mr. St. Rock, your eight thirty appointment is here. Max Stone," his secretary said. "Ok, send him back," replied Boston.

"Hi. I'm Max Stone your new attorney," Max said, as he smiled and extended his hand to Boston.

"Hi, I'm Boston St. Rock. The owner," Boston replied.

It was apparent that both men had a few things in common. They were both well-dressed, well-manicured and good looking men. As they sat down for their meeting, Boston paused the conversation to summon his brothers Austin and Bronx to the meeting. "Hold on before we start. I need to see if my brothers have anything they want to go over with you."

Boston called his secretary to have her page his brothers. In an effort to get to know his new attorney, he engaged in small talk to get a feel for the type of man Max was. After all, there were many attorneys to choose from in the city of Chicago. Boston had already met Max's father. But now he needed to get to know Max.

Boston was a man who got straight to the point, "So, have you handled large complicated accounts successfully?" Boston asked. "Sure I have. I've been taught by the best. My father would have it no other way," replied Max. "I like and respect your father. He convinced me in one meeting to switch lawyers and go with his firm. I hope you don't let me down," replied Boston. "I won't Mr. St. Rock," replied Max. "Call me Boston," he said.

As the small talk continued, Austin and Bronx entered the office. "Hey. Meet Max Stone. He'll be handling our companies' legal needs moving forward," said Boston. Both brothers shook Max's hand. "Did either of you want to talk to him about anything or are you good?" Boston asked. "I'm good," both brothers stated simultaneously, as they exited. "Nice to meet you Mr. Stone," replied Bronx as both brothers left the large luxurious office to return to their separate meetings.

Boston and Max wrapped up their meeting within just a few hours and it was obvious that the men had bonded. They were comfortable with the new partnership they would embark on. Boston felt confident that Max could handle *Rockwater Technologies* and Max liked and respected Boston. Max was sure he would prove himself the man for the job. As he exited the office, Boston extended an invitation of drinks and hors d'oeuvres at his brother Phoenix's lounge. Max asked where the lounge was located and promised Boston he would be there.

Before he left, Boston asked Max to look at a document he forgot to go over with him. "Can you take a look at this deal? I forgot to go over this one with you," he asked.

"Sure. I'll review it tonight," replied Max.

"It's kind of important. I want to give them my decision by Monday," Boston said.

"No problem, I'll go through it tonight. I'll call you if I see something that concerns me. See you tonight," Max said, as he left.

It was six o'clock and Boston and four of his brothers were headed to the lounge for an evening of drinks and socializing. Max was already there, sipping on Louis Cognac, and whispering in the ear of a beautiful voluptuous blonde. Boston walked in and spotted Max. "Hey Max, I see you got your hands full already," he said with a grin. Max smiled at Boston and the two engaged in more conversations of women, family, money and their plans for the future. They were quickly becoming friends. They had mutual respect and admiration for each other and it showed. They discovered other things they had in common. They both felt like they'd known each other forever.

As the night moved on, both men were feeling quite good after sipping on cognac all night. They were just about ready to call it a night when Max looked at Boston. He gave Boston a sly grin as he walked towards the men's room with the blonde following right behind. Boston knew what the look meant.

Max was in the rest room for a half hour and Boston got concerned. He didn't want his brother Phoenix to walk in on any improper situations. His brother had a classy establishment and Boston knew Phoenix would throw a fit if he knew people were openly fucking in his bathroom. Boston proceeded to the bathroom, Gurkha cigar in his mouth and a glass of Cognac in his hand.

As he got closer, he heard the moans of the young woman. Boston entered to find Max fucking the woman, doggy style, across the bathroom sink. "Come on man. You taking too long. Phoenix is going to fucking kill me if he finds out," Boston said. Max pulled away from the women, zipped his pants and kissed her on the cheek. He walked over to Boston and asked him if he wanted anything from the young lady. "You need something to set you up for the night? She's cool man. She's a lawyer working at this big firm downtown," exclaimed Max. "Naw man I'm good," replied Boston. "Go home. Sleep off that cognac. I'll get with you Monday," Boston said. "Yeah man. Alright!" replied Max.

Boston didn't engage in romps in bathrooms or quickies by the side of the road. He was much more refined than that. Boston respected women and pursued relationships not trysts. He had his share of meaningless sexual encounters, but that was never something he sought out to have. Boston wanted to be in love. He was newly single after breaking up with his girlfriend over her not wanting children. Boston wanted it all. The wife. The kids. And the fairytale ending.

Boston and Max talked several times over the next few days. The two men continued to bond with talks of going on vacation with their girlfriends. They made plans to travel to Miami for a quick weekend getaway. Max took the time to briefly tell Boston about Rose. Max refrained from going into too much detail, only mentioning that he was in a serious relationship. Boston, in his blunt and to the point manner, asked Max about his risky behavior.

"Why run the risk of fucking women you don't care about when you have a woman at home?" Boston commented.

"It's nothing man. They mean nothing. I love my girl Rose. You know how it is," Max replied.

Boston didn't understand. Unless Max's woman was the cheating kind or if Max was no longer in love with her, he didn't get the way his new friend spread himself so thin. Max was wealthy. He could get himself in trouble with his behavior. Boston was aware that there were women who would seize the opportunity and make false claims in order to reap financial rewards.

Boston changed the subject back to their possible Miami trip. He was long overdue for a trip that wasn't centered around business. They had thrown around the idea to take a weekend trip to either Florida or California, to party and have fun. The men were bonding quickly, as if they'd known each other for much longer.

"Will you be bringing your girl if we go or do you have another lady friend in mind? I can get my secretary to secure first class seats on a flight soon," he said respectfully. He didn't want to appear to be meddling too much in Max's personal life.

But Boston was perplexed. He didn't understand why Max was fucking strange women in bathrooms when he had a woman at home. "I'll probably bring Rose. She been a little suspicious of my increased travels these days. I don't need her to start not trusting me," Max said.

"But why do it? What's the point? I mean… It's your business man. I'm just saying…You put yourself at risk. Someone could scream foul. Try to take advantage. You know what I'm saying," Boston said, still trying to make sense of Max's personal life.

Max was beginning to feel uncomfortable with Boston's questions. The questions were making him feel guilty and Max didn't like to feel guilty about anything he did. "I love her more than I've ever loved anyone. I just get attracted to other women sometimes. It's fleeting though. They can't hold a candle to my Rose," replied Max, as he suddenly remembered he needed to call his father.

"I got a call to make. Can I call you later?" Max said.

"Yeah. Hit me up when you get a chance," replied Boston. Max thought no more of the conversation after the call ended. He didn't hold onto things for long. He knew his lifestyle was questionable and didn't care about anyone's opinion of it. For Max, the way he saw it, people wished they had his life even if they didn't want to admit it.

Chapter Four – The Encounter

Sunday afternoon was a relaxing day for Boston. He usually went to church with his family and then relaxed at home with a drink. He liked Sundays. He tried not to do anything work related and enjoy his time eating a home cooked meal prepared by his personal chef. The menu for the night was Lobster, asparagus and baby potatoes which was his favorite.

But this Sunday was different. Boston was getting worried because he hadn't heard from Max yet. The last time he talked to Max was Saturday morning and Max told him that everything looked ok so far. That he had just a few more things to go over and that he would call him. But Boston needed to get the documents for his meeting in the morning. He wanted to make sure there were no issues within those last few pages Max spoke about.

Boston picked up the phone and called Max, but Max didn't answer. Boston had Max's home number as well and tried him there. The phone rang several times before Rose answered. "Hello," she said, in her usual soft voice. "Hi. I'm looking for Max. Is he available?" asked Boston. "No. He's not here at the moment. Who's calling?" Rose asked. "Boston," he replied. "He won't be back until tomorrow morning. He had an emergency meeting and had to leave town," replied Rose.

"What! Out of town! He's got some important papers of mine," Boston said, his voice tense.

"I'm sorry. I don't know anything about papers. I can try calling him but I already called him about something else and he never answered," Rose said.

"Can you call him again for me. Please! I really need those papers," he replied. Rose promised Boston that she would call Max.

Rose made several calls to Max over the next few hours to no avail. Max was hundreds of miles away resting from a night of drinking and the hour long fuck session he'd just had. Rose was beginning to be suspicious of Max's trips and unanswered phone calls. She began to wonder if Max was having an affair.

He's always home at night. When would he have time. Other than his business trips, we're together too much for there to be another woman. Something isn't right though. I can feel it. He hasn't answered any of my calls. I better call Boston back, Rose thought.

Rose called Boston to deliver the bad news. "Hello," she said, as he anxiously answered.

"Hi. Did you get him?" Boston asked.

"No. I'm sorry," replied Rose.

"Damn! I need them by morning. Can you try to locate them?" he pleaded.

"I'm sure he left them there. He told me he would review them at home over the weekend," he continued. Rose agreed to look for the papers.

"Hold on. Let me look," she replied.

Rose went straight to Max's office which was in complete disarray. It was the only room in the condo where the door remained closed. Max had papers everywhere, but on his desk was a single folder with a stack of papers inside. Rose grabbed the file.

"What's the name of your company?" she asked.

"Rockwater Technologies," replied Boston.

"Oh, it's here. I found it. He had it on his desk," replied Rose.

"Oh, that's great! Can I swing by and get it?" he asked. Rose hesitated.

"Sure," she replied.

Boston hung up the phone after getting the address from Rose and jumped in his black custom Range Rover headed to Max's condo.

****

Boston pulled up slowly. He wasn't sure where to park. He hadn't confirmed with Rose if she would be bringing the papers down to him or if he was supposed to go up to the condo. Boston called the condo phone and waited as the phone rang over and over. He hung up, waited and redialed the number. He let the phone ring longer but Rose still hadn't picked up. Boston started to get worried. He didn't want to leave empty handed. He needed those papers and he was determined to get them.

What is going on? Boston thought. *I just talked to her, she knew I was on my way.* Boston refused to give up and called Rose again. "Hello," she answered. "Hi it's me. I'm here. I'm in the parking lot. Should I come up?" he said. "Yeah. If you don't mind," Rose replied. "I don't mind. What's the condo number?" he asked. "Unit 409," Rose replied.

Boston, dressed in True Religion Jeans a crisp white tee and Converse tennis shoes, walked toward the condo with purpose. He wanted the papers but he couldn't help but be intrigued by Max's significant other. He liked Roses' voice. It was soft, sexy and alluring. He was anxious to see what she looked like. What Boston didn't know was Rose was watching him from the window. She stared as he walked toward the building. She could barely see his face, but she definitely saw his physique. And she definitely noticed that he had a sophisticated and sexy way about him. He didn't walk, he glided. He had a powerful presence and Rose saw it four floors up.

She had been crying over Max and she didn't want Boston to see. She ran to the bathroom and looked in the mirror. *Oh no! My eyes!* Rose thought, as she wiped her eyes. Her eyes were blood shot red from crying. *Damn! I don't want him to see me like this. He'll tell Max. I should dim the lights as if I was preparing to sleep. It's late, he won't suspect a thing.* Rose ran through the condo cutting off all the major lights leaving only the plug-in night lights on.

Boston rang the doorbell. After just a few seconds Rose opened the door. Boston stood there for a minute, silent, staring at Rose. He was mesmerized. He was speechless for the first time in his life. Rose stood captivated by the handsome stranger at her door. They were locked into one another for a brief moment, and then Boston broke the ice, "Thanks for letting me come get my papers." Rose, still at a loss for words, smiled and nodded. "So, you have the papers?" Boston said after noticing that Rose had nothing in her hand. "Oh yeah. Sorry. Come on in. I'll get them," she said.

Boston entered and looked around. He liked the condo. It was nicely decorated and showcased the fact that Max was no slouch. "It's in here," Rose said, as she walked toward the office. Boston's eyes dropped down to Roses' ass, as she walked down the hall. The image held him spellbound. "Excuse the mess. This is the one room he refuses to keep clean," Rose said, as she approached the door. Rose opened the door and cut on the light. Boston walked over to the desk and grabbed his file.

As he turned around, he saw Roses red eyes. "What's wrong?" he asked, in a concerned voice. "Nothing. Just tired," Rose replied, as she looked down attempting to hide her eyes. Boston knew those were not tired eyes but didn't want to make her more upset. He could tell she was shy.

Boston walked slowly towards the door of the office, unable to take his eyes off of her. His mind raced as he tried to come up with the right words to say to her. He didn't want to leave. He wanted Rose. He wanted to know why she was crying. He wanted to kiss her and tell her not to be crying over Max. Boston knew that the out of town trip Max was on, probably involved another woman. Something about Rose made him want to take her in his arms. Boston started thinking that it would be better it he left. *I better get out of here. I want this man's girl. This is not right. I better leave now!*

"Well thanks," Boston said, as his mind raced. He was not ready to leave but he felt awkward. Rose smiled at him. She wasn't ready for him to leave. "You're welcome." Rose said, as her mind raced as well. W*hat the fuck. Why am*

I lusting over this man? I don't lust over men. I didn't even lust after Max, ever. What is this? Why do I want him? This is insane.

Boston walked towards the door to leave. As he walked past the kitchen, he could smell food she had put in the oven. "What did you cook that smells so good," he said. "Oh, nothing really. Just some shrimp pasta and garlic bread. You want some? You're welcome to stay and eat. It will be done shortly," she replied. *Rose what are you doing? Max would kill you. He can't stay for dinner*, she thought.

Boston turned around and smiled. "Yeah. I can't pass on that. You got it smelling too good in here." Rose smiled back at Boston and walked toward the kitchen. Boston followed closely behind, his mind still racing. *She's so fucking beautiful. Make up something and go now. This is not good. Max will not like this shit at all.*

Boston and Rose sat at her kitchen table while they waited for the food to get done. They ended up talking for hours before they even ate. Then talked even longer, while enjoying the meal she had prepared. Boston spoke of his personal life, his family and his upbringing. Rose told Boston things about her past that Max didn't even know. She was surprisingly open with Boston but she never mentioned Tina.

She told him about a couple of men she dated before meeting Max and how she and Max moved in quickly after dating. She spoke about her grandmother and her humble and reclusive life.

"Is Max the one? Do you think you'll marry him?" Boston asked. Rose hesitated. "I'm not sure. I mean... We haven't been together long. Maybe?" she said. "It doesn't take long," Boston said, as he looked at Rose. Rose paused. "Why aren't you married? You're handsome and successful. Women must throw themselves at you. Haven't you met that special someone?" she asked. Boston stared at Rose briefly then replied "Yeah I have. She just doesn't know it yet."

Rose smiled at Boston to hide the jealousy she felt. He was a woman's dream man and she felt that any woman, who had his attention, was lucky. But there was also a part of her that felt he had a thing for her. "You should tell her," she replied, then nervously got up from the table. *Who is this special person he's speaking of? He didn't mention anyone in particular when we were talking about our personal lives. Was that directed at me? It felt like it,* she thought, as she put their dirty dishes in the sink. "Well, it's getting late," she said. "Yeah. I guess I better go. The food was good and so was your company," he replied, as he walked toward the door. "Thanks again I really appreciate you letting me come so late to get this," Boston said, as the two walked towards the door.

As Rose opened the door, Boston looked at her. "Max is lucky to have you," he said, looking intensely at her. Rose smiled while trying to keep her composure. Her mind was going a mile a minute. The look in his eyes made her want him. What he'd said made her want him. But Rose didn't want him to see he affected her. That she was desiring him. "Have a good night," she said.

Rose shut the door and sat down on the plush oversized couch in the living room. There she sat, in the dark, staring out the window. She was blown away by her feelings. She had just spent four hours with a man she had never met. A powerful connection had just occurred. She was strongly attracted to Boston and was now fantasizing about fucking him. Rose put her feet and continued thinking about him until she fell asleep.

Boston's drive home was an unsafe yet uneventful journey. His thoughts of Rose were so self-consuming, that it affected his driving. He almost missed his exit and he ran a red light. When he finally arrived home, he entered his luxurious estate and threw his keys on the table. Boston was walking extremely slow and deliberate, pacing himself, because he was still heavy in thought. *What the fuck just happened?* he thought. He was more confused than ever about Max's life. *How could he have a woman like that and not be with her every waking moment?* Boston tried to shake off what he was thinking and feeling. But he couldn't, all he could see was Roses' face.

Chapter Five – Yearning

The next few days were a bit of a fog for Boston and Rose. Max had made it back from his trip, to a quiet and withdrawn Rose. She told Max she was on her period in order to get out of sex with him. She couldn't have sex with him. She had to wrap her head around what was going on. She had feelings that she couldn't explain for a man she had just met. Max was totally oblivious to the events that had occurred as he spoke with Rose,

"Did you see a file. I thought I had left it on my desk in the office?" he asked. "Oh yeah, your client called and said he needed it. I let him come and get it," Rose said. "Oh! Well ok. He was in here though," Max said, in a slightly jealous voice. "No. I took it down to him. He pulled up and I just gave it to him," replied Rose. *Why am I lying to him? I have never lied to Max,* Rose thought.

Max went into the family room to relax and watch something interesting on tv. "Hey Rose. Want to go get something to eat?" Max asked, as he flipped through the channels. "No, not yet. I'm not hungry right now. Are you hungry? I could fix you something," replied Rose. She didn't want to leave out. Rose was comfortable and had a lot on her mind. "No. I guess not. Maybe later. Just wanted to make sure you were good," Max stated. "Yeah. I'm good," replied Rose, as she opened her laptop.

Max's phone began to vibrate. "Max, your phone is ringing," Rose said, as she sat at the dining room table looking up recipes on her laptop. Max jumped up to get his phone like he always did. He didn't want Rose to glance down and see a woman's name. He guarded his phone like a soldier on a private reserve. "Oh, it's Boston," he said. Without thinking Rose lit up and smiled. She hadn't had time to control her reaction. She hoped Max didn't catch it. He hadn't. He was still tired from his travels and wasn't really focused on anything.

"Hey man. What's going on?" he said. Max continued to talk to Boston as Rose tried to listen in. She tried to discern what Boston was saying. His voice sounded muffled and wasn't clear. She was only able to hear what Max was saying.

"Yeah man. I just got back," Max stated, pacing the floor as he spoke with his client and friend.

Max continued his conversation with Boston as he walked from the kitchen into the living room. "No, I'm not going to be able to go. I have another business trip that I have to go on with my father soon." Rose rolled her eyes at the thought of another business trip. But deep down, she didn't care. Rose realized that she actually wanted him to go. She wanted the trip to happen sooner than later. She was hoping he wouldn't suggest that she go with him.

I hope he doesn't ask me to go. I don't want to go and I don't want him to touch me before he goes. This will be the longest menstrual cycle ever, Rose thought. Rose always shut down sexually on Max whenever he irritated or upset her. His back to back trips were unwelcomed in their already touch and go lives. "Let's plan it a month from now. Ok, that's cool man. I'll talk to you later," Max said, as he hung up the phone.

The two hung up and Boston stood shaking his head. He immediately began to think about Rose. *He's going on another damn trip. This muthafucka. I swear. He doesn't deserve her.* Boston sat at his desk going over some of his upcoming projects as he continued thinking about Rose. He'd fantasized about her from the day they met. He wanted her. She was possibly the one. The woman he wouldn't be able to live without. Boston wanted Max to plan the Miami trip. He wanted to see Rose, even if it meant in the presence of Max on a trip. Boston would do anything, just as long as he could be around her again.

Boston knew that he couldn't just go back over to Max's condo and he couldn't just call and talk to Rose. His mind raced as he tried to devise a plan to see her again. He made excuses, as he attempted to rid himself of the guilt he felt. He was lusting after Max's woman and there was nothing he could do about it. *He couldn't possibly love her the way he says he does. He doesn't deserve her. I shouldn't feel bad about what I'm feeling, I barely know him, I owe him no loyalty. Besides, I felt something from her,* Boston thought.

Boston tried to stay focused on his project but was too distracted to concentrate. He stopped working and went to the office lounge to get a cup of coffee. His anxiety was obvious and did not go unnoticed. His niece, who was working as a secretary, looked at him with bewilderment. *Coffee! When does he ever drink coffee while he works,* she thought. But Boston felt like he was coming unglued. He wanted to see

Rose. He needed to look in her eyes once again. He needed to see if what he was feeling was real.

The words of his grandmother played over and over in his head. He remembered the talk they had about women. The advice she had given him as a young man in his early twenties. His grandmother had told him to stop chasing girls. She went on to tell him that he would know when he met "the one." She told him that he would get an intense feeling about the young lady from the moment he looked into her eyes. She told him that love at first sight was real. That he should look for that experience and not settle for just any woman.

Boston had always held on to that belief. He trusted his grandmother. She was a wise and strong woman. A woman of great character, who never compromised her values. When she died, Boston made a promise to himself to follow her advice and not marry prematurely. To only marry his soulmate.

Boston had another project that needed legal review before he could go forward with the deal. He picked up the phone and rang his secretary. "Can you get Max Stone on the line for me," Boston asked. "Sure, no problem Mr. St. Rock," she replied. A minute later his secretary phoned, "Mr. Stone is on the line for you," she announced. "Great! Send it through," he said.

"Hey Max. How's it going?" Boston said, as he fiddled with his pen while reviewing the papers in front of him. "Hey. Nothing much. Out with my girl making a few runs," Max replied. Boston placed the pen in his mouth and bit down on it. He was jealous but tried to keep his composure. "Oh yeah. Well I was calling because I need you to review something I'm working on. I need your opinion before I finalize anything," Boston said. "Oh, I'm not that far. I can stop by and grab it. I'll review it tonight and let you know what I think by morning," Max replied. "Ok, great. See you soon," Boston said, as he hung up.

Boston immediately thought of Rose. This was it. His opportunity. She was in the car. Max was on his way. Boston jumped up from his desk, as excitement took over. He was surprised at how open Rose already had him and he hadn't even kissed her. He had to know if what he was feeling was real. He'd never felt this way before. He had his pick of women. Some of the most beautiful women in the world. Why her and why now.

Boston paced the floor, overwhelmed by his feelings. *He's got her with him. Ok, stay cool,* he said, as his thoughts raced. Boston could see the street from his third-floor luxury office suite window. He continued to pace the floor while looking down at the street as he eagerly anticipated her arrival. *Stay calm*, he thought. It wasn't long before Max pulled up in his white Range Rover.

Max did not immediately exit the car and Boston could see Rose sitting in the passenger seat. He could tell that they were engaged in conversation as she looked back and forth between Max and the building. Boston wanted to see Rose up close. He realized that Max would probably leave her in the car and come into the building alone.

Boston dashed though his office, file in hand, trying to reach the car before Max exited. He walked down the hall and towards the elevators, nervous yet excited. He was anxious to see her. To look at her. He hadn't stopped thinking about her since they'd met. The night they laughed and told each other intimate details about their lives. Personal things. He wondered if she wasn't just flirty. Something told him she wasn't. But he still needed to see. He needed to look into her eyes. He wondered if she thought of him. His grandmother told him the feeling would be mutual. That he would know. That his intuition wouldn't lie to him. His grandmother's face was vivid in his mind as he thought of her sound advice. He was on his way to see if he was right. In one night, he had fallen in love with a woman he barely knew and he wondered if the feeling was mutual.

Boston didn't bother to take the elevator and ran down the stairs. As he walked towards the entry door, he could see that Max was still sitting in the car. Before Boston could get to the door, Max emerged from the car. The two men stood in front of the building smiling and exchanging handshakes. Boston did not want Max to catch him looking at Rose and initially kept his eyes on Max. Boston handed him the contract and Max started glancing over it, line by line. Max occasionally looked at Boston and commented on some of the information. Max pulled his pen from his shirt pocket and started making small marks where he needed to review closer. "Is this your only copy? I need to make a note," he said. "No. Go ahead," Boston replied, as he stood there.

Boston glanced over at Rose but she was looking straight ahead at that moment. Max asked Boston about the details of the initial agreement. He could see that the copy he was given was a revised version. Boston told him how the original deal made him uncomfortable. He wished to retain the rights but preferred to lease the technology for a specific period of time. Then when he was ready, he would release it to an open market later.

The two men talked as Rose occasionally glanced over at them. Rose was nervous at first. She didn't want Max to see her staring at them. But she was glad that she had a chance to see the man who captivated her in one evening. She had thought of him non-stop and this was her opportunity to see him again. She had no idea when she'd get another chance. He was new in Max's life and Max wasn't one to have men over to his condo. She knew she wouldn't get the chance again and so Rose looked at Boston.

She watched him as he spoke with Max. As he explained his dealing and what his contract was to include. He was dashing. Better looking than any man she had ever laid eyes on. He had style and a presence. He was sexy and she wished she had fucked him. Maybe then she could forget about him and not think about him every day. But something was wrong. He didn't look at her. She waited. And waited. She felt he would. They had a brief but intense meeting and something magical happened that night.

Why is he ignoring me? she thought, as she became upset. *I cannot let this man affect me. I barely know him. He probably has someone and just didn't want to mention it. Besides, that's Max's friend,* she thought.

Rose sat in the car staring at Boston. There he stood, in a dark grey, sophisticated suit with a lavender colored shirt and matching print tie. Boston was looking like a million bucks and Rose now knew she had to have him. Max's friend or not, there was something about their connection. Something about that night that could not be ignored. She was completely smitten with him and she desperately wanted him. He was the first thing she thought of when she woke up and the last thing she thought about before she went to bed. She wanted him sexually. She knew that her relationship with Max was in trouble. It was possible that Boston was that other half. The half Elouise had told her about.

Several more minutes had gone by and Boston hadn't looked at Rose. He felt vulnerable standing there. He couldn't take the risk of being caught staring at Rose. He didn't trust himself. One look and he was sure Max would be able to read into it. Max continued turning pages, as he quickly scanned the documents.

"Well. Just glancing at these, I already spot a few problems. I'm going to have to go through this deal carefully," he said, as he looked at the final page. Boston seized the moment and finally looked at Rose but could only see her side profile. He continually glanced up at Rose as he spoke to Max about the specifics of the deal, but she never looked back at him.

"That's why I needed you to get right on it. I'm uncomfortable with some of the wording," he said, as he watched Max read over the pages. Boston turned his attention back to Rose. He was confused. There was something about her demeanor. She seemed sad. Something wasn't right. Boston started to wonder if maybe her and Max had an argument. He didn't understand the look of pain on her face. The look of disappointment as she looked ahead. Even from her side profile, he could tell she was in a mood.

Boston stood there with his hands in his pockets, staring at Rose. He was sure he felt something that first night they met, yet she wouldn't acknowledge him standing right in her face. *Why won't she look?* he thought. Boston had abandoned any fear of being caught by Max. He wanted Rose to look at him but she never did.

"Ok man, I'll hit you up later. I'll finish reviewing this tonight and I'll highlight what needs to be re-worded or removed altogether," Max said, as he walked toward the driver side of the car. "Yep," Boston replied, disappointed that Rose was distant. Boston stood there as they pulled off, in a trance. Rose could see him in the rear-view mirror. She watched him until his silhouette faded into obscurity, unaware of his desperation to connect with her.

Rose was eerily quiet on their ride home. "You ok baby?" Max asked. "Yeah, I'm good. Just tired," she replied. Rose was confused. She didn't understand why Boston didn't come over and speak to her. Why he wouldn't even look at her. Max reached out to hold her hand but she pulled away. Max thought that Rose was upset because their day got interrupted with business. "I know you don't like when I mix business with our one on one time. It won't happen again," he said. "It's fine Max."

"Hey listen, I have to go on another trip in a few days. I won't be gone long this time. Maybe three days at the most. Will you be alright until I get back?" Max said nervously. He knew that Rose was growing tired of his ever-increasing business trips and wondered if she was beginning to suspect anything.

"I'll be ok. Just leave me some money before you go. I want to shop and we need groceries. We're running low on food," she said. Max spoiled Rose and gave in to her requests. He liked to keep her happy and his lifestyle afforded him the ability to indulge her. Rose did not abuse Max's generosity and only occasionally made such request. But Max was overly generous with her. He always gave her more than she needed, in an effort to keep her and keep her happy.

Max packed his bags for his flight. He had just a few hours to get ready. He was always particular about what he took and needed hours to pack for just a couple days of travel. He packed his best jeans, athletic wear and knits for the brisk evenings. He also made sure to grab his favorite Audemars and Chopard watches from his watch case. His trip to New York was going to be an exciting one. He had made arrangements for the female attorney he fucked at Phoenix's lounge, to join him.

Rose entered the bedroom to check on him. "You need help packing?" she said. "No baby, I'm almost done. But I need you before I go," Max replied. Rose knew what he meant. She still had on her night gown and no underwear underneath. Her usual at home attire. She looked at Max then proceeded to the bed and laid down. Her manner was that of a woman doing a duty rather than making love to her man. Max disrobed and laid on her. He kissed on her face and neck, caressing her body slowly. Max continued kissing her slowly as he made his way down her body. He didn't want to appear to be rushing, but Max also knew that Rose loved to have her clit sucked.

He knew he could not give her some *wham bam thank you mam* quickie and then leave for three days. So, he made sure to do all the things he thought would please her and keep her content until he returned. Rose enjoyed the lovemaking and moaned in ecstasy as he slowly licked and sucked her. He made his way up to her breast and began to kiss her passionately as he fucked her slowly and deliberately for the next twenty minutes.

Max jumped in the shower, got dressed and rushed out the door for his flight. "I'll see you in a few days babe. I'll call you when I land," Max shouted, as he shut the door. Rose laid in the bed for a few minutes, deep in thought, as she stared at the ceiling. She reached over to her dresser and pulled her vibrator from under a stack of underwear. She'd recently purchased it and was keeping it hid from Max for the time being. She didn't know how he'd take her having a vibrator. Rose knew that Max thought she was having orgasms with him.

Rose began to play with herself while rubbing the vibrator on her clitoris. It wasn't long before she was climbing the walls from her intense orgasm. *Wow, this thing is phenomenal,* she thought, as she lay there breathing heavily. Rose closed her eyes and fell asleep. She had exhausted herself but she was content, for the moment.

*B*oston was preparing to rest for the night. He had not heard from Max since giving him his latest project to review. Max had dropped it off at Boston's office a few days before but hadn't called since. *I wonder if he's gone on that trip he talked about. What about Rose?* he thought. Boston lay in his bed, restless, thinking of Rose as the sound of hard rain beat against his window. He usually slept like a rock in this type of weather, but not this night. He wanted Rose and it was affecting him more and more.

Boston picked up his phone and called Max. "Hey Boss. What's up," Max answered. "Nothing much. Just need you to review something for a meeting I got coming up," Boston replied. "Aw man. I can't. I'm out of town right now. Won't be back until Sunday night," replied Max. "Oh, ok. It's cool. Call me once you're back in town," replied Boston. "Ok, I will," Max said, as he hung up.

Boston hung up. He hoped that Rose was in town, alone. He arose out of bed and paced the floor, in the dark, contemplating what to do next. *Should I just call the condo and see if she answers?* he thought. *But what should I say? What if I'm wrong? What if she tells Max?* His mind raced. Boston picked up the phone, dialed the number and abruptly hung up. "I can't do this. I could be wrong," he said to himself, as he walked around his room. *Fuck, man. I don't care. Maybe if I fire his ass, I'll stop feeling so fucking guilty.*

Boston picked up the phone and called again. He let the phone ring several times, then hung up. "She must be with him. Maybe that's why she's not answering," he said. He sat on the bed and held the phone. He knew that if he was to ever find out how she felt, it was now or never. Max could come home and not do another trip for months. Boston was not prepared to wait any longer. Every day not knowing was eating away at him. *I have to call. I have to find out. If she tells him, then so be it. I don't need him. I don't have that type of loyalty to him. Not when it involves her!*

Rose sat in the bathtub with tears in her eyes, ignoring the rings of her phone. She was mad at Max, upset about Boston and wrapped up in her emotions. She heard the phone ring, but sat there motionless. She needed to unwind. She needed to get herself together. She thought it was Max calling to check in on her. Rose was outdone at the audacity of such a move.

How dare he continue to go out of town, leave me home then stalk me while he's gone, she thought, as she laid back in the warm water. Max had been on more business trips than Rose cared to admit to and she was growing suspicious of them. He would call her constantly then the calling would end abruptly. She had a feeling that he was calling her at specific times when he was away from whoever he had gone on the trip with.

Most of his calls were during the day and maybe one call, in the middle of the night. The call she believed was just to make sure she was home and in bed. Rose sat there in the tub and closed her eyes briefly, picturing Boston's face. Her tears were replaced with a warm, embracing feeling. She was mad at him for what she considered to be his disregard of her. But she couldn't help but forgive him. She didn't want to be mad at him. She wanted to know him. She longed to get closer to him.

What are you doing Rose? What about Max? Boston has someone. A man like that would not be single, she said to herself. Rose felt guilty. She had strong feelings and desires for one of Max's clients. His new friend. The person that he was working with and building a friendship with. *I have to stop thinking about him. This is crazy!*

Boston sat down on his chaise, looked out the window and contemplated his next move. He wondered should he just give up. *It's now or never*, he thought. He didn't want to be wrong and face the embarrassment and fallout that would surely come if she rejected him and told Max. *I'm not wrong though. I know I'm not. She's waiting on me to say something first*, he thought. *My grandmother told me I wouldn't be wrong. That I would know, that I would feel it.* Boston called the condo again.

"Hello," Rose answered, in a melancholy tone. "Hello," Boston nervously replied. "Yes," Rose said, unaware at that moment, of who was on the line. She knew it wasn't Max's voice. She wasn't sure who would be calling at that time of the night. Boston held the phone for a minute as he gathered his thoughts. Rose took the phone from her ear to look at the caller id. She was shocked to see the name *Boston St. Rock* on the receiver. A rush of emotions overwhelmed her. Rose looked over at the clock, it was one thirty in the morning. She could hear noise in the back ground and knew he was still on the line. "Hello," she said again, nervously.

"Hi. It's me, Boston," he said. "Oh... hi," she softly replied. "Did I wake you?" Boston asked. "No, not really. I was just lying here. I hadn't fallen asleep yet," Rose replied. Boston became silent again. His anxiety had stolen his words. He thought for a moment. He paused as he gathered his thoughts. Weighing his words carefully and seizing the moment Boston said, "There's something I need to ask you. Something I need to know. It's been on my mind and...." Boston paused as he began to fear her response. Rose closed her eyes. She knew what the call was about. All his hesitation and rambling. His long pauses and delayed responses were due to one reason, but Rose wanted him to say it.

"Just say it," she replied, opening her eyes and staring at the ceiling. Boston took a deep breath and said, "I've been in love with you since the moment I met you Rose. I know it's wrong with me knowing Max and all, but I am. I can't stop thinking about you. I just can't," he professed. Rose smiled. She wasn't ready for that much honesty. She had no idea he would use such powerful words. Rose put her head under the pillow, held it tight, and replied, "Me too."

Boston was in shock. He could not believe what she had just said to him. He was excited. He knew it. He felt it. It was just as he had suspected. Just as his grandmother had said. She did feel the same way. She didn't hesitate letting him know. This was his moment. He didn't think of right versus wrong. He didn't consider that another man would have his heart broken. The only thing Boston knew was that he loved an unmarried woman and that he was going to go and get her.

She was not Max's wife so he felt even less guilt. He believed that if it was meant for her to be with Max, they would have never connected the way that they did. He threw on some jeans and a tee shirt and dashed out of his house headed to see her. Rose was quiet, holding the phone and holding her pillow even tighter. She couldn't believe what they were saying but she was relieved she had told him. She was in love with him and she was ready for him to know.

"I'm on my way," Boston finally said after a minute of silence. Rose sat up. Her eyes got big. Her heart started pounding. She sprung up and ran to the bathroom. "Ok, call me when you're outside," she replied nervously. *What! Did he just say? On his way? I look terrible. Oh no. I'm not ready to see him yet. On his way for what? This is not happening. What about Max?*

Rose hurried, as she tried to prepare herself. Boston was calm during his drive to see Rose. He felt as though a huge weight had been lifted and he was determined to get her. He wasn't sure how he felt about going over to Max's place but he had come to terms with the decision. He knew that after this night, there would be no more Max Stone and that he would end up with Rose. He had to. He was in love with her.

Boston pulled up and called Rose. "Hello," she answered. "I'm on my way up," he replied. Rose instantly got nervous but she was ready. She was ready for whatever was about to happen. She didn't care anymore. Boston knocked gently on the door then leaned against the frame. He waited a few agonizing seconds, desperate to see her face. He tried to control his lust for her. He'd had dreams of what he wanted to do to her. She was everything to him. She turned him on like no other woman ever had. But Boston was fully aware that it was more than lust. He found her intriguing. She had a good heart and was open with him. It was more than sex for him.

Rose was already standing at the door. She thought of what opening that door for him meant. She knew he was there to claim her. That he would be unstoppable. His aggressive and take-charge personality was apparent the first time they'd met. Rose took a deep breath and then opened the door slowly. She stood there staring at him intently with a lust in her eyes that made him push her against the wall.

Boston kissed her fervently, as she moaned and held on to him. He guided her body to the wall just inside the doorway and shut the door. Rose pulled up her gown and then took his hands and guided them up her body. Boston grabbed her by the hips and pulled her to him. "Boston," she moaned, as she took his hand and placed it on her pussy. She had on a night gown and nothing else, which aroused Boston instantly.

Boston held her face and kissed her soft and passionately. He played in her hair and rubbed her lips with his thumb and then stuck his thumb in her mouth. Rose sucked his finger in such a passionate way, that he almost ejaculated. He had so much pinned up excitement, that he almost came prematurely, something he didn't do.

They continued kissing in the foyer and Boston picked Rose up and walked over to the couch. He slowly removed his clothes and lay on top of her. Rose could barely contain herself. She had never felt this way with Max. She moaned and squirmed as Boston sucked her neck, then moved slowly down to her breast. He was a passionate and generous lover with tender yet strong kisses. He had Rose going out of her mind. He used his hands to stimulate her, as he kissed all over her body. He made his way down to her waiting womanhood and nibbled her gently. He sucked on her intensely for nearly a half hour and Rose came, hard. Rose was in shock. *What just happened? Did I just come? Are you fucking kidding me? I love this man.*

Boston worked his way back up Roses' body, kissing on every part of her and she squirmed and moaned in ecstasy. He then used his hand and began to rub her clitoris. As Roses' moaning became more intense, Boston finger fucked her slowly, as he dove his tongue in her mouth. Rose came again. *Are you fucking kidding me?* she thought. Rose just looked at him. She couldn't believe he had made her come twice. She had underestimated Boston. His strength was that he paid attention, especially when he was in love. And as he touched her in certain areas, if she reacted a certain way, he knew to increase that action. He knew not to let up.

Boston looked into her eyes and said, "I love you." Rose smiled. "I love you too," she replied. Boston then kissed Rose deeply and passionately, as he gazed into her eyes more intently. Rose kissed on Boston then went down on him. Something she desired to do since she first saw him. She took most of his dick in her mouth, which made Boston squirm. He couldn't contain himself. Rose had skills, and Boston couldn't take it anymore. He snatched her up and flipped her over and began to fuck her hard and deliberate.

Rose initially pulled away because of the size of his cock, but then began fucking him back. Boston started whispering in her ear as he fucked her steadily. "I love you and you're going to have to leave here tonight. You're coming with me. Forever. You not coming back here. Do you hear me Rose?" Boston said.

"Yes," she replied. "I love you. I belong with you," she whispered.

Boston began to fuck Rose harder and faster as she begged him to stop. She had come hard and couldn't take his dick any longer. But he refused to let up. Boston came right after she did and they both lay there staring at the ceiling.

Rose was trying to gather her thoughts and get herself together. She was in disbelief after the deeply intense lovemaking session they had just had. She was ready to go with him and not look back. *I'm going with him. I have to. I love him,* she thought. Boston was playing in her hair as she laid on his chest. "Come on we should go," Boston said. "What should I grab?" Rose asked. "Nothing."

Chapter Six – Catalyst

Max walked briskly through the airport, nervous and sweaty, headed toward gate number 11. His flight back to Chicago was leaving in fifteen minutes. He'd left his companion behind at the hotel in his haste. She was given money and a kiss and told to return home at her convenience. Max had told her that something urgent had come up and that he had to get back to Chicago quickly. Gate 11 seemed miles away and Max's anxiety consumed him.

He had not heard back from Rose after leaving her numerous voice messages throughout the night. And now her phone was off. Max wondered if perhaps Rose was aware of his out of town rendezvous and was angry. He boarded the plane and sat there, starring out of the window hoping that he wasn't too late. *I hope she hasn't left. Why would she cut her phone off? This is so fucked up,* he thought. This was unlike her. She always returned his calls. Max ran through every scenario. *What if she's left for good? What does she know? Has Ashley told her anything?*

"Hi sir. Would you like anything to drink or perhaps a snack?" the flight attendant asked. Max looked over at her. His mood quiet and melancholy.

"I would like a stiff drink. Something strong. Do you have Vodka?" he asked.

"Yes, we do. Will there be anything else? Breakfast will be served soon," she said, wondering why the handsome gentleman was so despondent.

"No thanks. Just the drink," he replied.

Max was gripped in fear and worry. He didn't want to lose Rose and of all the worst-case scenario's playing out in his mind, Ashley speaking to her was at the top. Max was sure that Ashley was cool and wouldn't try to break them up. Ashley was Roses' closest friend and he couldn't imagine her doing anything to jeopardize that. But Max couldn't contain himself. His fears were beginning to take hold. This was going to be a long flight home.

***

Standing in the great room, looking out the window, Rose stared at the trees rustling back and forth. She was feeling a mix of emotions about what had just occurred. She's in Boston's house, in Boston's tee shirt thinking about Max. Rose didn't like the way she was leaving things with Max. She didn't want to hurt him. She didn't want him to be devastated and she knew that he would be. *I've got to talk to him at some point. I can't leave things like this. He deserves better*, she thought. But she didn't want to face him yet. Rose put on the only clothes she had. She didn't bring anything from Max's condo and had nothing but a pair of jeans and a shirt.

Boston gave Rose money to go shopping and to get a new cell phone before he left for work that morning. He had also left her with the keys to his car. She took her time to start her day. She listened to music, as she slowly made her way thru Boston's house getting familiar with the layout. It was a huge six-bedroom estate. She loved the beautifully designed home. But as she walked through the house, trying to get herself together, her mind kept returning to thoughts of Max.

Rose walked toward the kitchen and made a cup of coffee. She sat down on the tall stool in front of the kitchen island and sipped slowly. She recounted the events of the night before. She remembered the long quiet ride back to Boston's place. She remembered his attempts to comfort her and how she remained quiet during the ride. But Rose was happy to be with Boston. She blushed when her mind went to thoughts of the wild, rough sex they had all through the night. She daydreamed about the long hard thrusts Boston gave her as he whispered how much he loved her in her ear. How he gently sucked her nipples and then slowly kissed her stomach before spending the next thirty minutes eating her pussy.

Boston had skills and he was good at reading body language from a woman while fucking her. He knew when to fuck hard, when to ease up, when to slow down and when to speed up. There wasn't much he wouldn't do and even licked Roses' ass, something she never experienced. Rose came multiple times whenever she made love to Boston.

Boston fucked in a more animalistic way than Max did and Rose was completely turned on by that. He liked to pull her hair with just the right tension and he enjoyed putting his hands on her throat. Rose loved it. Boston liked it rough and she had a few love bruises to show for it. He was able to make her have orgasm after orgasm. Boston was a better lover than Max and Rose was sprung, but she was still in love with Max.

I guess I'll go shopping first, then head to momma's, Rose thought, as she got into Boston's Range Rover and headed towards downtown. Rose had plans to meet up with Boston for lunch around noon. As she drove towards the shopping complex, her phone started to ring. "Hello," she answered. "Hey baby. What you doing?" Boston asked. "Hi baby. I'm going to this boutique to get a few things and then I'm going over to momma's house. What about you? I'll still be there by twelve," she said. Boston told her about his busy morning and the issues he was having with his brother Denver. Denver had gotten himself in yet another office affair and it had ended badly.

Rose and Boston were casually talking when Roses' phone line clicked. It was Ashley calling. "I have to take this bae. It's Ashley," Rose said. "Ok baby. But you need to be on your way though. I need to see you. I miss you already," replied Boston. Rose smiled and relished in the attention Boston was giving her. She was insatiable when it came to him and wanted to be with him. "Ok, just give me a minute. I'll go to mommas then be on my way," replied Rose. "Ok, call me soon," he said. Rose hung up from Boston and answered Ashley's call.

"Hello," she said. "Hey girl where you been? I haven't heard from you," Ashley stated, in a concerned voice. "I know. I'm so sorry. I've just got a lot of things going on. I was going to stop by and see you, but I got to head downtown. What are you doing tomorrow? Let's have lunch. I'll come and get you," Rose said. "That's cool but tell me now Rose. What's going on? Are you in some kind of trouble?" Ashley asked. "I don't know Ashley. It all happened so suddenly. I can't get into it now, plus I want to see you. It's too much to go into. I'll come get you tomorrow," Rose stated. "Ok girl, you take care. Whatever it is, it will work itself out. Don't you worry. See you tomorrow," Ashley replied.

***

Max entered the condo, laid his keys down on the table and began looking around. He quickly made his way through, going room to room, hoping Rose had fallen asleep in one of them. Max became frantic when he saw Roses' phone laying on the kitchen counter. He knew that she had to be with someone because all of the cars were still there. *She's with someone*, Max thought. *But who?* Max jumped in his

Camaro and sped off. *I'll try her grandmothers first. Then Ashley's. Where else could she be?*

He drove by Elouise's house and circled the block. He wasn't sure he would be welcomed there. If Rose was angry and went there to get some time to herself, he wasn't sure how she would react. Max contemplated what to do. *I'll just knock on the door. She's got to talk to me,* he thought, as he circled back.

Max went back around to Elouise's and knocked on the door. "Yes," Elouise said, speaking through the door. "Hi it's Max. Is Rose here?" he asked. Elouise opened the door and smiled at Max. "Oh hi. It's certainly nice to see you again. Rose isn't here. I haven't seen her today," she replied.

Elouise liked Max and thought of him as a complete gentleman. She had only met him a few times prior, but she had a good feeling about him. "Do you want to come in?" Elouise asked. "No mam. I was just trying to locate Rose. But it's nice to see you," Max said. "If I see her, I'll tell her to call you," she replied. Elouise watched as Max walked to his car and pulled off. Max drove away still confused about what was going on. He had an unsettling feeling. *Something's up,* he thought.

*B*oston sat in his office talking with Denver and Bronx about an upcoming venture he wanted to get started on. He was in the process of making a gadget to attached to cell phones. He wanted it to work by plugging the phone into a computer, while the call was in progress. The technology would allow the person to see who they were talking to on the computer or television screen. "I think it's a great idea. Once we work out the issues on we can get the computer and television manufacturers on board. We should have this off and running in no time," Bronx said.

Bronx was older than Boston and Denver. He was the second born son of Orlando and Cicely St. Rock. Bronx was handsome, charming and sophisticated. He taught his younger brothers how to dress and conduct themselves when it came to business. He was trustworthy and reliable and the family respected him immensely. His siblings relied on him for advice when their personal lives were in shambles. He was the most stable and loyal of the St. Rock men. Even his own father reached out to him when there was a crisis. Without his level-headed way of thinking and his influential ways of dealing with people, *Rockwater* would have faltered. It was Bronx who talked to many of the would-be, lawsuit seeking women and got things under control. He was invaluable.

Denver was two years older than Boston and was a whiz at computers and other forms of technology. But unlike Bronx and Boston, Denver was more unpredictable. You never knew what you were going to get with him. He was an extremely handsome, twice divorced father of six. His looks did not go unnoticed by women.

He was the source of a lot of the sexual misconduct allegations against the company. He would embark on a heated romance with one of the employees, abruptly end the affair and eventually have the woman fired. His behavior had cost the company millions. Boston had warned Denver after the last lawsuit and Denver had been keeping a low profile ever since.

"Yeah that's going to be a hit. I can help with the prototype," Denver said. "We will need at least one computer company to be on board. They need to make the necessary changes to the board and the processing unit. We also need one of the cell phone companies to get on board. Once we have one, they will all want the specs. But of course, we'll have to give exclusive rights to one of them first," Denver stated, looking at his brother. He started reading the specs that Boston had drew out and prepared. "Yeah, I know. But we're slightly behind schedule on this one. I need you working overtime on this," replied Boston.

Boston looked at his clock. It was time for him to meet up with Rose. "I got a lunch date fella's. I have to go," Boston grinned. "What? With who?" Denver asked. Boston smiled at the thought. It was more than a lunch. It was time with his baby. A woman that had him completely, as if she had been there the whole time. "You'll meet her later. I'm bringing her to momma's dinner party," Boston said, as he grabbed his phone. His brothers stood up to go back to their offices. Bronx and Denver spoke briefly about another project as Boston checked over his schedule one last time. "When is momma's dinner. I forgot about it. Heather probably hopes I forgot. She been on some bullshit again," Bronx said, speaking about his wife. Denver and Bronx left out of the office as Boston prepared to leave.

***

Ok, I'm going to run in here for a second. Boston's probably already on his way to the restaurant, Rose thought, as she pulled up to her grandmother Elouise's house. Rose knocked on the door and Elouise answered. She was happy to see her granddaughter. Elouise immediately alerted Rose. "Max was by here not too long ago, looking for you." Roses' eyes got big. Max had never come over to grandma Elouise's house by himself before. But she wasn't surprised. She knew he'd be looking for her. Rose knew that Elouises' would be the first place Max would go.

Rose tried to keep her composure. She didn't want Elouise to suspect there was trouble between them. "Oh, really. What did he say?" she asked. "Nothing! Just that he was looking for you and to ask you to call him," Elouise replied. Rose kissed her grandmother goodbye and quickly left. "I'll see you later ma. I got a few more runs to make," she said. Rose headed towards the restaurant to meet with Boston. She had tears in her eyes. She was emotional. Rose knew that this was no way to treat Max. She knew she had to call at some point and explain to him what happened. She tried to pull herself together. She didn't want to reach her destination crying because she knew Boston would assume that she was upset over Max.

Rose walked into *The Sea Bass*. A well-known seafood restaurant that sat off the water with fantastic views and some of the best food in town. Boston stood up from the table and kissed Rose as she approached him. "Hi baby," he said. "Hi," Rose replied. Boston ordered crab cakes and mashed potatoes. Rose ordered Salmon, couscous and fresh diced tomatoes with lemon pepper.

As Rose sat there having a wonderful lunch with Boston, she started contemplating going to go see Max. She knew that Boston had to go back to the office and that she would have a few hours of free time. As they wrapped up lunch, Boston asked Rose to follow him home. The look on his face suggested he wanted to make love to her. "Ok. But don't you have to go back to work?" she asked. "Yeah. But I have time. I miss you when I'm not with you," he said. "Ok. But I have a doctor's appointment, so we can't be all day Boston," Rose said, hoping that he would make it a quickie so that she could go see Max.

***

I need to talk to Ashley. Damn! She's going to want me to stay if I go over there. But I've got to go. I've got to see what she knows, Max thought, as he drove towards his condo. *Fuck it, I'm going.* Max turned completely around and headed for Ashley's house. She lived in the same neighborhood as Elouise. Max had been living with a terrible secret that Rose was not aware of. He fucked her best friend Ashley shortly after moving Rose into his condo and felt terrible about it. He tried to distance himself from her, but Ashley was aggressive and constantly made herself available to him.

Max always had a hard time saying no to women who threw themselves on him. He'd regretted approaching her at the center where Rose used to work and talking to her about Rose. He wished he could take that day back. He had been living in fear ever since he started with Ashley. She had something on him and he never knew if she would grow tired of the situation and expose them.

"Who is it?" Ashley said in a sweet, delicate voice. "It's me," Max replied. Ashley opened the door and kissed Max on the lips. She could tell by the serious look on his face and his lack of enthusiasm that something was definitely on his mind. "What's wrong?" Ashley asked. "I need to talk to you. It's about Rose," he replied. Ashley was just glad to see him, they had only hooked up a few times and she wanted to see him more. But she could see that something was bothering him. "Oh. Well come in," she said.

Max hesitated. He wanted to have the conversation on her porch. After a moment, he reluctantly entered and sat down on her couch. Ashley sat next to him hoping he was not there to end the affair. "Rose is gone," Max said, in a somber voice. "She left me. Do you know why?" he asked. "No Max. I don't know anything. She called me and said she had something to tell me. But she refused to talk about it over the phone. We're supposed to have lunch tomorrow," Ashley stated, as she looked away in disbelief.

She was shocked Rose left. She was sure Rose was too much in love with him to just leave. "You haven't told her anything have you?" he asked. "Of course not Max. I wouldn't do that," Ashley replied. "I want to know where you're supposed to meet her. I want you to call me as soon as you know. Don't tell her I asked," he said. Max stood up and kissed Ashley on the cheek. "I'll call you later," he said, as he left.

*****

Boston and Rose returned home from lunch and wasted no time removing their clothes as they hurried towards the bedroom. Boston walked up behind Rose, bent her over the bed and entered her from behind. He held her head down as he entered her. Rose enjoyed his aggressiveness and managed to break free from his grip and turned over so he could lay on her. He was an awesome kisser and she liked to kiss him while he fucked her. They made passionate love for almost an hour.

Boston fell asleep on top of Rose and she laid there holding him close. She'd thought of waking him but didn't. She knew he wasn't sleeping much and wanted him to get some rest. *I need to talk to Max. He must be frantic, trying to find me. What if he thinks something happened to me? Plus, I have an appointment. I need to wake him soon.*

Rose lay there for a half hour then began stretching her legs and her movements woke Boston. "What time is it? Oh shit, I got to get back to the office," he said, as he got out of the bed and hurried into the bathroom. Boston showered, dressed and rushed back to work. Rose lay on the bed, deep in thought about whether she should call Max or go to see him. She thought that Max deserved to hear it from her face to face. But she was ashamed and wasn't sure she could face him. She decided she wouldn't tell him over the phone. *I'll go over to Max's place later when I think he's there.*

Rose got up and took a quick shower. Her cell phone began to ring. It was Boston. "I forgot to tell you that my mother is having a dinner party soon and I want you to go with me," he said. "Ok baby, of course. That'll be nice. I get to meet your family," she replied. "Ok. Love you babe I'll call you later, I'm going out after work for drinks with my brother's," Boston said. "Ok. I'll see you when you get home."

"Max, are you here?" Rose yelled, as she slowly walked through the condo. It was six o'clock in the evening and she was hoping he'd be there. She made her way through each room, calling his name. Max was nowhere in sight. When she reached the bedroom that she had once shared with him, an overwhelming sense of loss took hold. She sat down on the bed as tears began to stream down her face. She laid back on the bed and stared at the ceiling. Rose closed her eyes and just laid there. She could smell Max's cologne. *Where are you?* she thought.

Rose lay there for nearly an hour, gripping and smelling his pillow. She thought of how they first met. She thought of the center she used to work at and how she missed the children. Rose missed her life. She wasn't sure she liked the direction her life was taking. She loved Boston too, but she wasn't sure if she'd made the right decision. *We moved too fast. I should have made him wait and took the time to work things out the right way. But it's too late now. He's all in and he will be hurt too if I told him how I feel,* Rose thought. Rose wiped her tears, grabbed a bag and filled it with as much of her belongings as she could. Before leaving, she sat at the kitchen table with paper and pen in hand and wrote:

Max. I am sorry for leaving and not saying goodbye. I can't stay. I have decided to move on and I wanted to tell you. I wish you were here. I didn't want to leave like this. I probably don't deserve you and I do feel bad about all of this. Love, Rose.

Her drive back home was one filled with emotion as she tried to pull herself together. She pondered her future. A future she thought she would have with Max and now was ready to have with Boston. She hoped that Max would move on. She knew this would devastate him. But she hoped in time, he would forgive her. She didn't want them to be on bad terms. They were too close. They were bonded. He plucked her from obscurity in a humdrum life and gave her the world. And for that, she would be eternally grateful. *What's done is done. I can't go back now. I will always love him. Always!*

Chapter Seven – Honeymoon Phase

Life seemed good in Boston St. Rock's household. His projects were coming along as planned. His family was good. His woman was happy and he couldn't be better. Rose was comfortable with Boston and had gotten to know his family. She'd met everyone at the dinner party Cicely's threw for her children and everything seemed ok. She had concerns about some of his brothers'. The men were flirty and she wondered if Boston picked up on it. There was also one brother that was no stranger. She had met him before. But Rose decided she wouldn't let anything interrupt her and Boston's life. Rose could see that Boston was close to them. She worried that anything she said about them, would cause a rift between her and him.

She struck up a friendship with his sisters and his mother Cicely. The St. Rock family liked Rose and was glad to see Boston happy. Five months had gone by since Rose had tried to see Max. She still thought of him but she had moved on. She'd spoken to Ashley a few times but realized it had been a few weeks since their last call. Ashley seemed to be avoiding her calls and that was unlike her.

"I'm gone baby, call me when you get up. I might be able to meet you for lunch if I'm free," Boston said, as he was preparing to leave for an appointment. "Ok," Rose replied, as she lay in the bed relaxing. Rose lay there for a few hours and eventually got up to fix herself something to eat. Boston's sister Tacoma was on her way and was calling Rose to see if she was free. "Hey girl what you doing? Can you go shoe shopping with me? Neiman's got a nice selection," she said. "Yeah, I guess. I'm not doing anything else. Boston is too busy to do lunch so I'm free," Rose replied.

Rose enjoyed her day out with Tacoma. She was building a relationship with all of Boston's sister's but Tacoma was more outgoing and had went out of her way to get to know Rose. The two women talked about everything. Rose was careful not to mention too much about her past. She gave vague responses when asked about her immediate family, only mentioning Elouise. Tacoma opened up about her youth. She told her what it was like growing up with so many men under one roof. Tacoma was slight in appearance but she was strong, fierce and independent. She learned those traits watching her brothers.

The women enjoyed their shopping trip and were ready to call it a day. "When's your trip to Puerto Rico?" asked Tacoma. "We're leaving in two weeks. We'll be gone for seven days. I can't wait," Rose replied. "We have plans to go to Jamaica too. Aren't you supposed to be going on that trip?" Rose asked. "Yeah. Definitely! I'll be there. Me and my girl," Tacoma replied.

When they arrived back at the house, they were surprised to see Boston there with brothers Denver, Dallas, Memphis and Austin. The men were drinking Cognac and talking about what was going on in their lives. The St. Rock brothers were close and kept up with one another. "You talked to mom today?" Tacoma asked Memphis, as she walked into the great room. She was happy to see her brothers. "No, not yet. I just got back in town. I'll call her later," he replied.

Memphis was a handsome yet tough man and was a fierce protector of his family. No one messed with him. He had a reputation and could be dangerous if a situation got sticky. "Where you two been?" asked Boston. "Shopping," replied Rose. Rose smiled and spoke to everyone then went over to Boston and hugged him. He kissed her on the cheek and then continued his conversation with his brothers.

Austin, an architect by trade who also worked at Rockwater, smiled and greeted Rose and his sister. Dallas chimed in "Tay, why you always at the mall? Did you leave anything for someone else to buy?" he jokingly said to his big sister.

Dallas was one of the younger brothers. He was twenty-two and liked to kid around a lot but he looked up to Boston and was protective of him. He was handsome and charming like his older brothers and was fond of Rose. All the brothers were, but they knew to keep their place. Most were married or otherwise engaged and besides, she was their brothers' girl.

Tacoma was aware of her brothers' past competitiveness when it came to women they were interested in. They had been known to pass women between them, especially if the relationship was not serious. When one would end it, the other would begin. But they were grown men now and this type of behavior was no longer tolerated. Their women were off limits to one another.

Tacoma and Rose retreated upstairs to look at what they had purchased. The two continued talking for a few hours. "Well girl, I better get going," Tacoma said, as she stood up from the bed. "Ok. Thanks for coming to get me. It was fun. I'll call you tomorrow," Rose replied. As she put away the new items she purchased, she ran across a tee shirt that Max had gotten her on a trip to Florida. She balled the top up and put it back in her drawer then closed her eyes and began to think of him. She was overwhelmed by her feelings once again and grew more anxious to talk to him. She stood there for a few minutes then opened her eyes and saw Boston standing there watching her.

"What's wrong? You feeling ok?" he asked. "Not really," Rose replied. "Well come lie down. I'll get you something warm to drink," he said. Boston walked with Rose over to the bed and then went to the kitchen to get her some tea. He laid down next to her, cut the tv on and stayed by her side for the rest of the evening.

The next morning Rose got up and made her way to the kitchen. "I made some coffee and toast. You want some?" Rose said as she prepared her coffee with cream and sugar. Boston rushed past her, worried he would be late for a meeting. "Yeah. I got to make it quick. I have to get going," he replied. "I'm going to be working at that center I told you about. I start Monday," gushed Rose. Rose had recently contacted the family center where she used to work, to enquire about volunteer work. She was getting bored and needed an outlet. "Ok baby. Whatever you want," Boston smiled.

He walked over to Rose and started to kiss her. He kissed her passionately and then kissed her on her forehead before heading out. They had made love all morning and Boston was running late. They had only been back in Chicago a few days from their trip to Jamaica with some of Boston's siblings and their significant others. Rose hadn't unpacked yet and wanted to relax. Her phone began to vibrate. It was Ashley.

"Hey Girl. Where have you been?" Ashley asked.

"Nowhere," Rose replied.

"I haven't talked to you. Are you mad at me or something?" she asked.

"No. Why would I be? I've been busy. I'm about to start volunteering at the center and working with the kids again on Monday," Rose replied, excited she was back at the center.

"You should. You always loved it there. I didn't tell you but I'm not there any longer," Ashley said.

"What? Since when?" replied a surprised Rose.

"I don't know. Maybe a month. I'm at a restaurant now. It's good money. You would know all this if you called sometimes. You're just scared I'm going to pry and ask you about your personal life," Ashley said.

"We'll talk I promise. But I have to go. I'll call you ok?" Rose was not ready to tell Ashley what was going on. Ashley wasn't good at keeping secrets and she knew it. Rose needed to leave for a doctors' appointment and to meet with Mr. Sullivan about her schedule and responsibilities for the upcoming weeks. *I'd better get going.*

***

The doctor's office was filled with women waiting to be seen. Rose sat there and flipped through magazines, patiently waiting her turn. Rose was patient but she was also worried. She had a battery of test ran to check her female reproductive parts. She wanted to know if she would ever be able to conceive or carry a child.

Years prior, Elouise had broken the news to Rose that doctors said she would never have children. The news devastated Rose and she went into seclusion for months only leaving her house to go to work. She barely remembered the act that left her so badly damaged. She was now finally able to face her fears and look into her reproductive health. She had blocked out a lot of her past and had tried to put it all behind her. She wanted to be a mother. She was hoping that her body healed itself well enough to make that dream come true.

"Ms. Walker," the receptionist called. Rose stood up and entered through the door and was escorted to a private room. She waited nervously, shaking and biting her nails. She closed her eyes and listened to music from her cell phone. Music always relaxed and calmed her.

"Hi Ms. Walker," the doctor said, as she entered the room. Rose opened her eyes and cut her phone off. "Oh, hi Dr. Nichols. Sorry. I was trying to calm my nerves," she said.

"Oh you're fine. So, I'll get right to it. As you know, we ran the tests. I looked at your results and even had them looked at again by a specialist. The images show you have a lot of scar tissue on your uterus," The doctor stated. She continued explaining to Rose her findings.

"Well. The damage…Well, it's extensive. We just don't see how you will be able to carry a baby. Your eggs are fine. Your ovaries are intact. It's just your uterus. You could get a second opinion if you like. I could refer someone," the doctor said, as she looked at Rose with concern.

"No," Rose said, so softly that it sounded like a whisper.

"I'm really sorry," the doctor replied. "Come to the front desk and I will have my receptionist give you the name of several specialists we use. Just in case you change your mind."

****

Rose was emotional on her drive to meet with Mr. Sullivan about volunteering. She wanted to turn around and go home. But she needed this job now more than ever. It would give her the chance to bond with children and make a difference in their lives. Even if she could never have her own. *Pull yourself together Rose,* she thought as she pulled up.

"Mr. Sullivan, nice to see you again. It's been a long time," Rose said.

"Yes, it has. You look more beautiful than ever. Life must be treating you well," replied Mr. Sullivan.

"Yes, I'm good. Thanks," Rose said.

"So, I made out a schedule for you. Take a look at it and let me know if it works for you. I tried to pick the days we have more staff here, so that you'll stay busy," Mr. Sullivan said, as he handed Rose the paper.

"Thanks Mr. Sullivan. I still start on Monday, right?" Rose asked.

"Yes. I have you down for Monday working with Ms. Adams. We have a new outdoor playground for the children and she will need help supervising them. It's just a few hours twice a week for now," Mr. Sullivan said. "We can include art classes if you decide you can volunteer more hours later," he concluded.

"Ok," Rose agreed.

Rose was happy to be starting back at the center. She loved children and enjoyed caring for them. It always made her feel important and needed and it was something she never had. *If I can't care for my own babies, I guess I'll care for someone else's.*

"Hey pop," Max said, as he entered his father office. "Max. You can't work from home on all matters. Some things require your presence in the office son," Max Sr. stated. "I know," replied Max. "You missed a very important meeting with a new client. I had to bring Jeff in on it and he has his hands full. I need you to get up to date on the newest companies' legal needs. We meet with them again next week," asserted Max Sr. "Yep," Max said, as he headed towards the door. "Where are you going now?" said Max Sr. "Home," Max replied. Max went to his office to grab a box that Sherilyn had filled with cases he was working on.

Max had stepped out of the forefront and was acting more as a consultant to several of the attorney's in the firm. Sherilyn cared for Max deeply and always had his back, even if she over stepped the boundaries at times. "Max. If you need anything else, just call me," she said, as he was leaving. "Thanks, Sherilyn". Max's phone rang as he walked to his car. It was Ashley. He hesitated at first but answered.

"Hello," he said. "Hey it's me. I know you're busy but I…" Ashley said, but was abruptly cut off by Max. "I can't talk right now. I need to call you back," he said. "But it's about Rose," Ashley stated quickly, trying to inform him of what she knew before he hung up. Max stopped in his tracks and stood there motionless. "Max are you there?" she said. "Yeah. I'm here," he replied. "I spoke to her. I wanted to tell you that she starts back at the family center on Monday," Ashley stated. "Where she used to work. Wow. Ok," he said, as he ended the call. He didn't know what to think. He was excited, anxious, speechless and angry.

Max woke up earlier than he had in months. His demeanor was calm. He'd waited months for this day to arrive. He was finally going to see Rose. He wanted to talk to her. He wanted closure. If she had moved on with her life, he wanted to know why. Max thought of what he would say. He knew that if he approached her aggressively, she would just shut down on him. *I need to be calm when I talk to her. If I come on too strong, she'll just shut down and not talk.*

He watched the clock, on edge, waiting for it to read ten o'clock. It was nine forty-five and Max couldn't wait any longer. He left out and got in his car and pulled off. He was an emotional wreck as he drove to the center. He still loved her. She had broken him into a million pieces. As he continued to drive to the center, he became more emotional then became angry at himself for getting emotional. He didn't like the fact that Rose had this power over him.

He wanted to move on. He had fucked several women in an attempt to move on. But Max knew he was losing the battle. He still wanted Rose and he wanted to know what had happened. He blamed himself but he wanted to hear her say he was the problem so he could try to fix things between them. He believed strongly that she was aware of his cheating. If the break up was because of his philandering ways, he was prepared to stop. Nothing was worth him losing her. Nothing!

Max pulled up slowly at the center. It was quiet. There were a large number of cars in the parking lot. Max sat in his car looking around. He could see that there was a huge, newly renovated playground on the side of building. He remembered Rose used to tell him that after art class, she took the kids outside to play. Max decided to just wait in his car.

He was driving a new black Camaro with tinted windows. He had purchased it after wrecking his burgundy Camaro one day following a night of drinking. A night he tried to drink his problems away. He had been sitting there for just over an hour when the doors flew open and out ran a group of children. Following close behind was Ms. Adams and walking alongside of her was Rose. Rose was smiling and talking and directing the kids toward the playground.

Max got emotional when he saw her. He rolled his window down slightly so he could see her better. He sat there and watched her every move. He admired her beauty. The way she carried herself. Her smoldering sex appeal. Rose had noticed the car but didn't think much of it. But then she noticed movement in the car through the cracked window and started paying more attention. She stood there with her arms crossed as Ms. Adams walked up to her. "Who is that?" Ms. Adams asked. "I'm not sure," Rose replied, in a concerned voice. Just as the women stood there watching the black Camaro, the car abruptly sped off down the street. The car raced to the end of the street, bent the corner and vanished. Rose stood there dumbfounded. She had a sinking feeling and grabbed her cell phone to call Ashley.

"Ashley," Rose said, as she paced the yard.

"Yeah," Ashley replied.

"Hey it's me. Listen, I've got to ask you something. Do you know what kind of car Max drives?" Rose asked.

"Well, the last time he came up to the center he had a black Camaro," Ashley replied.

"Not Burgundy?" Rose asked.

"No. A new black one. He tore up the burgundy one," she stated.

"Ok, thanks."

Rose hung up and walked up to Ms. Adams. "After we get the kids back inside, I need to leave early," she said, talking at a fast pace and sounding worried. "Sure. Everything ok?" Ms. Adams asked. "Yeah. I just have something to do," Rose said, with a bewildered look on her face.

She knew that was Max and she wasn't sure what to make of his visit and then speedy exit. She wasn't sure how he knew she would be there. She suspected he may have asked Mr. Sullivan since he probably still made donations to the center. Rose wasn't sure what had just happened but she knew she had a strong desire to find out. Something came over her and she wanted to see him and she was not going to wait.

Max returned home solemn and disappointed at himself for not confronting Rose. He had gotten cold feet and pulled off in a haste when he saw her staring at the car. *What the fuck! She was there. Right there. I should go back*, he thought. Max went to his office and tried to take his mind off of Rose. He was fatigued. He hadn't been getting any rest since losing Rose. His work responsibilities had suffered. He was avoiding family and friends. His mother wasn't feeling well and that only added to his stress. His father seemed too busy to care and so Max had to fill in for his father. He took on the responsibility of getting his mother back and forth to her doctor's appointments.

I can't believe this. I should go back. She was right there, he said. Max felt a headache coming on and went to the bathroom looking for pain relief medicine. He took the pill and laid down on his couch waiting for the pain to subside. Max was calm as he lay there with the letter she wrote in his hand and staring at the ceiling. He cut the tv on and closed his eyes and began drifting off to sleep.

Rose stood over Max watching him sleep. She wondered why he didn't answer the door after she had knocked. Rose still had her key and Max had not changed the locks. She stood there with tears streaming from her eye as she looked at his hand. Max had the note she'd written to him clutched in his hand. "Max," she said softly, as she touched his shoulder. Max was startled and grabbed her hand as he awoke. He was frozen at the sight of her standing over him. He slowly arose and just stood there in front of Rose. No one spoke a word.

He reached out and grabbed her and pulled her to him. He held her tightly as he was overcome with emotion. "Why did you write me this note and then disappear?" he asked. Rose looked down in shame, unable to look at him. "I don't know. I tried to see you but then I couldn't face you," she said. "Were you mad at me?" he said then paused. "Wait! Is there someone else?" he asked, with a disappointed and emotional expression on his face. Rose hesitated then looked away. She looked back to him. "Yes," Rose said, in a soft voice. "Who?" Max asked, as he tried to keep calm.

Rose shook her head then looked down. She was not ready to divulge who she'd been seeing. She was filled with emotion. Max was her first love. But Boston was her first true love. The man she didn't think she could be without. The man who held her heart in his hand. Rose couldn't divulge this information. She could not state these facts. This would destroy Max. She couldn't destroy him. This was not his fault. This would have happened whether he had been messing around or not. Rose felt destined to be with Boston.

Max placed his hand on her chin and forced her to look at him and asked her again. "Who is it Rose?" he said. "Boston," she replied. Max became enraged. "What! How could you do that? When did you start fucking him? Why didn't you tell me?" he said, as he walked in circles, ranting and full of rage. "You mean to tell me that I've been calling that muthafucka trying to see why he hadn't needed my legal services and all this time it's because he's been fucking my woman. I thought you left because of me," he shouted. "What do you mean? Why? What did you do?" Rose replied. "Nothing," Max said, still enraged and not ready to air his dirty laundry just yet.

Max grabbed Rose then tore through the buttons on her shirt which turned Rose on. She grabbed his face and kissed him deeply and passionately. She didn't realize how much she really missed him and she wanted him, bad. She removed the rest of her clothes and Max began removing his. Rose laid down on the oversized couch. The same couch she fucked Boston on. As Max went to lay on her, she pushed him, rolled over and got on top of him. "I missed you so bad," she said. "I missed you too. I looked for you. I never stopped looking for you. You better tell him it's over," Max commanded.

Rose began to ride Max relentlessly. She tongue kissed him with fierce passion as she held on tight. He was turned on by her aggressive behavior but furious about what she had revealed to him. He pushed her off of him and rolled her over on her stomach. Max laid on her and entered Rose's ass with his penis. Rose yelled out at first then buried her head into the couch pillow. Max fucked her in her ass and didn't let up until she eventually pushed him off of her after a few minutes. Even though the pain was intense, Rose enjoyed his aggressiveness.

She turned around and laid on her back and looked at Max. "Do you forgive me?" she asked. Max shook his head no. He wasn't ready to forgive. He was mad at her. Mad at him. He wanted to kill Boston. Max laid on top of her and rubbed her face as he looked into her eyes. The pain he had went through was obvious and Rose was overcome with emotion. "I'm sorry for all of this. I should've come and talked to you. I still love you," Rose confessed.

Max kissed Rose and began to fuck her fervently as he squoze her cheeks forcing her mouth open. He dove his tongue in her mouth, kissing her with deep passion. Rose came right then as she moaned and screamed in ecstasy. Max tried to hold out. He missed Rose and didn't want to come too soon but couldn't help himself. The look on her face as she came made Max release. They lay there breathing heavy and relishing the moment as they dozed off from sheer exhaustion.

Max awoke and eased off of Rose. He didn't want to wake her. He quickly put his clothes on, grabbed his phone and left. Max was consumed with rage when he pulled up in front of *Rockwater Technologies*. He walked into the office and right past the secretary

"Um, excuse me sir," she said.

Max walked right past Boston's brother Denver and right into his office. Boston and Bronx were in the middle of a conference call when he barged in. Boston looked up and immediately hit the silent button on his call. He looked at Bronx and then looked at Denver who was standing directly behind Max,

"Give me a minute fella's," Boston said.

Bronx took one look at Max then looked back at his brother. "No! I don't think so. What's going on?" Bronx asked, as he looked at Max then back to his brother Boston.

The room went silent for a minute.

"Was you going to tell me you been fucking my girl? You meet me then you go after my girl?"

Denver looked at Boston in disbelief.

"Your girl?" Boston said, as he tried to keep his cool.

Max became enraged and began to shout. His voice lit up the office as he fumed. "You don't even know her muthafucka. You know nothing cause she ain't told you shit because she belongs to me."

Boston hung up from his call, looked at his brothers then looked back at Max. "Max. I can see that you're mad but I'm going to tell you this shit just one fucking time. She's not yours. Not anymore. And if you ever come to my office like this again, I'm going to put my fist through your fucking face."

Max walked toward Boston and Denver grabbed his arm. "Come on man. You gotta go. You know we're not going to let nothing go down with our brother. This is a no-win situation for you. So how about you just leave," Denver said calmly. Boston smirked at Max which infuriated him. "She's always been mine. That's why she's sleep right now. At my place muthafucka. That shit with you wasn't going to last. She'll always come back to me. So, stay the fuck away from her. And I'm going to say that shit just one time," Max warned.

Chapter Eight – Brotherly Love

*I*t was three o'clock in the afternoon when Rose awoke to an empty condo. She looked at the clock and panicked. She got up from the couch and yelled out Max's name. W*here did he go?* Rose picked up her phone and saw she had missed numerous calls from Max, Boston, Tacoma and Ashley. *Damn. Something's happened. Max!* she thought. Rose hurried and put her clothes on. *Oh shit. He tore my shirt. I can't wear this,* she said, as she walked down the hall. Rose went to Max's room and opened what used to be her drawer. She pulled one of her old tee shirts out and put it on.

As she walked out, she tried calling Max first but he didn't answer. Rose then tried Ashley. "Rose," Ashley answered hysterically. "What? What's wrong?" Rose replied. "Max is in jail. He went to some guy named Boston's office and the police had to be called," she said. "What! Who told you that?" Rose asked. "He did. He's been trying to call you. Even Tina called me," Ashley replied. "What?" Rose hung up on Ashley and tried Max's phone again.

As she repeatedly tried to get Max on the phone her phone rang, it was Boston. "Fuck," she yelled out. Rose was afraid to answer. She raced to get to his house. She wasn't sure what she would encounter. But she knew one thing for sure. That Boston would be there waiting. Her phone rang again. *Shit. I better answer*, she thought.

"Hello," she answered.

"Where the fuck are you?" Boston blurted.

"Um… In my car," she replied.

"Where are you coming from Rose?" Boston asked, obviously pissed off.

"Mommas," she replied, as her anxiety began to build.

"Don't lie to me. I just got into a fight with this muthafucka. You been fucking him Rose. You better come home now," Boston yelled.

"I am. I'm on my way now."

Rose pulled up to Boston's house. He was already there and was standing in the doorway with both hands in his pockets. *Damn he looks mad.*

Rose was nervous and took her time getting out of the car. Boston stood there looking heated as he waited for her. Rose walked slowly towards the house and opened the door. Boston stared at her as she walked in. He stood there in the doorway looking out as she walked past him. Boston continued standing silent in the doorway with his hands still in his pockets. "You mind telling me what the fuck you were doing over at his place?" he said. Before Rose could get her answer out Boston turned around to face her and yelled, "And why you fucking him?". His cadence changed and he calmly said, "Before you answer Rose, let me warn you. If you lie to me, this shit is going to blow up like the Godfather."

Rose burst into tears. She had never seen Boston like this and she was afraid. She didn't know what to make of his cold and calm demeanor. Especially, given the fact that he knew she fucked Max. She put her hands over her face as if to shield herself and said, "I don't know what happened. I just wanted to talk to him. I never got a chance to tell him bye and I always felt bad about that," she cried. "Why would you go back to him. He's fucking everybody including your best friend," he yelled.

Rose's wiped her face and just looked at Boston. She shook her head no. "Yeah. He is Rose. I've done my homework on that muthafucka. I know everything," Boston stated. Boston then got in Roses' face, looked her directly in her eyes and said, "If you go back. If you ever fucking go back. You stay." Boston put on his suit jacket and walked out the door. Rose stood there in shock, crying hysterically. *This is so messed up.*

***

Things calmed down over the next several weeks. Rose stayed in the house only leaving out to get groceries and run small errands for Elouise. Boston was keeping a *tight leash* on her and she allowed it in an effort to keep the peace between him and Max. Max Sr. bailed Max out of jail and Rose had not spoken to him since that fateful day. And Max kept his distant from Rose after he found out that she was back with Boston. Rose had not spoken to Ashley after Boston had revealed that Max was fucking her.

Rose started to put it all together. *That's why Max said he thought I left because of him. And that's why Ashley seemed so distant at times. And it explains how she knew so much about what was going on.* Rose played it all out in her mind. *I'm going to call him. I'm going to call her. I'm not just letting that shit go,* she thought, as she lay there next to Boston.

It was the middle of the night and Rose was restless. She hadn't had a good night's sleep in weeks. She wanted to confront Max and she wanted to confront Ashley. But Rose was afraid. She knew if Boston found out, things would fall apart at home. It was going to take time to build trust again with Boston and she didn't want to take any chances. But knowing Max and Ashley had been intimate, was eating her alive. She had to know for sure. She had to hear it from Max himself. *I'll call them tomorrow when I'm here alone,* she thought.

*****

Boston left out the next morning headed to work. He kissed Rose, left his credit card on the table and walked out the door. Rose had told him the night before, that she was going over Elouise's house and then shopping. Rose waited until she heard his car pull off and then called Max. It was a

Thursday morning and she knew he would be getting ready to leave for work. "Hello," Max answered. "Hey it's me," Rose said. Max paused then said, "Come over Rose. I need to see you. We need to talk."

"No Max. I'm not. That's not why I'm calling. Is it true that you're fucking Ashley?" she said. Max held the phone. He was nervous and hesitated answering her. "Max answer me. Is it?" she repeated. "No," he replied. "Yes, it is. Tell me the truth Max," Rose pleaded. "Where'd you here that at? Who said that?" Max stalled. "Max, I swear. I will click over and call Ashley and see what she has to say about it. You need to be a man and tell me the truth right now," Rose insisted. Max paused and began breathing heavily. Rose could hear him and she quietly waited for him to say something. "Yeah," he said somberly.

"What?" she said. "When? When was the first time Max? Is this a recent thing after I left or before?" she fumed. "Come here and I'll explain," he said. "No. I hate you right now. All this time I've been beating myself up thinking I had done you wrong when you deserved it all along. Why would you fuck my friend right under my nose Max?" Rose asked, as she sobbed. "Rose. Please. I need to see you. I'll tell you everything. Just come," Max pleaded. "I'm coming now and you're going to tell me everything," she replied.

Rose left Boston's home headed to Max's condo. During her drive there, she decided to call Ashley. "Hello," Ashley answered. "Ashley. You are not my friend. I know about you and Max. How dare you! You stay away from me and stay away from my family," Rose said, as her voice crumbled. She was in shock that Ashley had betrayed her.

"Wait Rose! I wanted to tell you. A lot was going on. I'm sorry. I didn't want to hurt you. Let's talk about it," Ashley pleaded.

"I don't want to talk. But I will tell you this. Max doesn't love you. He won't ever love anyone until he gets over me and that isn't happening anytime soon Ashley... I feel sorry for you," Rose said. She could hear Ashley sniffling before she hung up the phone. *Why would he do that. Why would she do that. I don't understand.*

Rose pulled up at Max's condo and sat there for a minute. Max had seen Rose pull up and was standing at the door waiting on her. He let her use her key and smiled as she entered. "I hate you still so don't smile at me right now," Rose said. Max walked up to her and starting playing in her hair as he always did. "I missed you Rose. I love you and I'm going to always love you," he confessed. Rose pushed his hand away and said, "How did you end up fucking her Max?"

Max drew closer and kissed her on the lips. He paused, weighing the backlash he would get as a result of being honest. Max knew he couldn't wait too long so he stepped closer to Rose and said, "It was a mistake. I was drunk Rose. She was at the same party I was at. It just happened." Rose started crying and Max tried to console her.

She pushed his hands away and Max grabbed her and started kissing her. Rose pulled away again. When Max grabbed her tight, she stopped fighting and laid her head on his chest. She closed her eyes and cried, as he continued to rub her hair. Rose always liked the way he held her and the way he smelled always turned her on. She remembered how she would sleep like a baby in his arms. And how he would lay with her and make her laugh until she fell asleep. Rose wanted Max. She missed him and she needed him.

She took Max by the hand and walked to the bedroom. He undressed her, looking into her eyes, as he slowly undid her buttons. "I want you back Rose. Whatever this is, we can work it out. You don't love him," he said. Rose began to feel guilty. She looked at him with intense passion. She did love him. But she loved Boston more. Max removed Roses' clothes and she slowly sat on the bed.

He pushed her back, pulled her onto the bed and lay on top of her. He didn't enter her immediately. He wasn't ready to make love to her. He just laid on her, playing in her hair and thinking of what else to say to her. He wanted her back from Boston. But he wasn't sure he could get her back, now that she knew about Ashley. "Rose. You don't know him. You don't know anything about him. You need to come home. This is where you belong," Max said. "I know," she replied.

Rose left Max's condo after staying the entire afternoon with him. She rushed over Elouise house to visit with her before she went back to Boston's house. "Hi ma. I missed you," Rose said, as she kissed Elouise on the cheek. "Hi baby. Where you been?" she asked. "Oh nowhere. Just staying in. It's cool out today. I've been in a lot more," Rose replied. "Well yeah. They say it's supposed to be cold all week" Elouise replied. "Yeah, I heard that too," said Rose. As the two were talking Tina knocked on the door. "Let your momma in. She just called and said she was on her way. That's probably her."

Rose unlocked the door and walked back into the living room. "Hey momma," Tina said to Elouise. "Hi honey," replied Elouise. "Hi Rosalee," Tina said, as she looked over at Rose sitting on the sofa. "Hey," Rose replied. Tina walked with Elouise into the kitchen where the two engaged in small talk. After a few minutes, Tina went back into the living room. "I got you something for your birthday coming up. I don't know when I'll see you again, so I got to give it to you now," she said. "Ok," Rose replied. Tina tried to sit down next to Rose but Rose immediately stood up.

Tina grabbed her daughter by the hand. "Why are you so mean to me Rose? I love you. I'd do anything for you," she pleaded. "Sure you would," Rose replied. Rose went into the kitchen and kissed Elouise. "I have to get going. I'll call you later," she said, as she walked towards the front door. She looked back at Tina then walked out. Tina watched Rose to her car. She stood in the doorway, her heart hurting behind Roses' dismissal of her. Elouise walked up from behind and stood next to Tina. "She'll stop being mad one day," Elouise said. "I don't know ma. I guess I messed up so bad in the past, that she can't see her way through it. I was really messed up then. She doesn't even know me now."

*I*t was time for Boston to get up and start his day. He and Rose had made love all night and he was tired. He woke Rose up with a kiss. "Hi baby. What time is it?" she said. "It's five o'clock," replied Boston. Rose stretched her arms and then rolled over on top of Boston. She started kissing him tenderly then slid under the covers. Boston closed his eyes as Rose sucked the life out of penis. She stroked him with her hand and took him deep in her mouth. Boston was large and difficult to take in but Rose knew how. She sucked and stroked him until he came in her mouth. Rose swallowed and came up and kissed him in the mouth. Boston lay there with her for a while as they talked about family and some trips that they wanted to take. "Speaking of trips, I have to go to New York. I leave Friday with Bronx and my father," he said. "Ok. When will you be back?" Rose asked. "We'll be gone for five days," he replied.

Boston got up and began to get ready for work. He jumped in the shower and Rose followed him right in.

"You're going to make me late for work. You know I can't take a shower with you without bending you over," he admitted. "That's not my problem," Rose whispered in his ear. Boston bent her over and fucked her hard and fast from behind as she held onto the shower bar. "Your phones' ringing," Rose said softly. "I'll call them back," he said, as he continued pounding her. Boston exited the shower and called the number back. "That's the office. I gotta go. The presentation I was working on has an issue. I'll call you later." Rose stayed in the shower enjoying the warm water running down her body. She loved the way Boston was with her and she desired him all the time. She couldn't get enough of him. She stayed in the shower touching herself and thinking of Boston. *Five days! What will I do without him for five days?*

***

Friday morning was like any other morning. The tv was on in the kitchen, music was playing in the master bedroom and the house smelled of coffee. Boston was still packing when his father showed up. "Hi darling. Where's my son?" he asked Rose, as she opened the door for him. "Still packing," she replied. "How you been?" asked Orlando, as he kissed her on the cheek. "Good. Would you like some coffee?" Rose asked. "Yes please," he replied. "Hey you almost ready?" Orlando asked Boston, as he walked into his son's bedroom. "Yeah. Just making sure I got what I need. Did you stop at the office to get all the documents?" Boston asked. "No. Bronx already picked everything up," his father replied.

The men continued talking as Boston finished packing his suitcase. Bronx pulled up and blew the horn. "Rose. Tell him we're coming," yelled Boston. "Ok," she replied. Rose opened the door and tried to get Bronx's attention. He finally looked up and then rolled his window down.

"Hi Bronx. They're just finishing up. They'll be out in a minute," she said, as she smiled at the handsome brother. Bronx smiled, waved and then looked down at his cell phone. Boston and his father walked toward the door with bags in hand.

"Ok baby. I left you money and a card. You have enough to do whatever you want. I'll call you when I get to the airport," Boston said. He kissed Rose and rubbed her face softly. Rose missed him already and he hadn't even left. She knew she would miss him. He was only going to be gone for a few days but she dreaded his not being there. "I love you," she said, as she kissed him goodbye.

The men walked out, loaded the Escalade with their bags and pulled off. Rose walked into the kitchen and started making breakfast. Rose thought of what she would do to keep herself busy. She was used to being with him every day. Making love to him every day. He hadn't left her for more than a day or two in the past and that had only happened twice. She was used to going with him when he needed to be gone longer. But she knew she wouldn't always be able to go and so she took a deep breath, exhaled and started her day.

Snow was coming down heavy the next morning. Rose looked out the window and watched as the thick beautiful snowflakes covered everything in sight. *I can't go anywhere in this. Oh well,* she thought. Rose sat around watching tv all day and shopping online. She tried to relax as she shopped for hours looking at different websites. She'd purchased two handbags, three pairs of Converse in bright spring colors, a coat and several pairs of jeans.

By mid-day Rose was bored and horny. She lay on the couch rubbing herself and staring at the ceiling. It wasn't long before she decided she wanted to masturbate and use her toys, which were in the master bedroom. Rose got up from the couch and proceeded to her room. She had on one of Boston's wife beaters and a pair of lace panties. She slid her panties off, grabbed her toys and laid in the bed.

Rose thought of Boston while she lay there rubbing her clit and fucking herself with a large purple dildo. Whenever she thought she was going to come, she would slow down. She didn't want to come too quick. She was horny and she wanted to come hard, so she wanted it to build up. Rose was moaning and totally consumed by what she was doing. She tuned out her phone ringing, the tv going and Denver, who was knocking at the door. Denver tried knocking for a few minutes. When Rose didn't answer, he decided to use his key. Most of Boston's siblings had a key for emergencies but no one had used their key since Rose had moved in.

Denver didn't trust Rose after what had happened at the office with Max. He had decided to check on the house and Rose. "Hello," he said, as he slowly walked through the first floor, looking around. He immediately got concerned as he could hear something but wasn't sure what it was. Denver walked up the stairs to check the bedrooms. As he walked down the hall, he could hear moaning sounds. The sounds grew louder and louder, as he approached Boston's bedroom. Denver was becoming upset. He knew Boston was out of town and he suspected Rose was fucking someone in his house. In his bed. Denver walked to the bedroom door, ready for whatever was going to happen. *Somebody's in the wrong place at the wrong fucking time.*

He peeked in the room and to his surprise it was Rose, alone. She was in the throes of ecstasy and was completely naked and playing with her pussy. She had laid her toys on the side table and was using just her hands. Denver's dick became hard as he watched Rose. He had never seen a woman masturbate in such an intense way. On porn maybe, but not in real life. He smiled as he stood there watching her. He backed up to make sure she could not see him and continued to watch.

Rose fucked herself with her fingers completely unaware that she was being watched, admired and desired. She tried reaching for her vibrator but it was too far away.

She opened her eyes and looked over at the table when something caught her attention. She was shocked to see Denver standing there. She gasped, grabbed the sheets and covered her body as Denver walked away. She sat there shaking her head, shocked by the site of him watching her. No one had ever seen her masturbate. It was something she did privately. *What is he doing here? Oh shit! How long was he standing there?*

Rose got up and slipped into her gown and looked out the window. His car was still there. *Damn, he's still here.* Rose wasn't sure what to make of Boston's older brother. Other than small talk at social gatherings at their families' estate, she hadn't really gotten to know him. She had only known one of the brothers from one of her rare outings with Ashley years ago. But Denver made her curious.

He was laid back and unassuming but his eyes spoke volumes. She had caught a few of his intense stares during the time spent at Cicely's house. He was obviously handsome and well built like the other St. Rock brothers. He seemed nice and was popular with the ladies. Even his family seemed to gravitate toward him. He had some similarities to Boston but was more laid back, more mysterious. Rose walked into the great room where he was sitting and sat beside him. They sat next to each other, not saying anything. Rose looked down. Denver looked around then glanced at her before looking away. He was afraid she'd tell Boston. But he also desired her and he was a man who was powerless to his desires.

"I'm so embarrassed," she said, as she looked straight ahead. "It's not your fault. I should've announced myself. I could have called out louder but I wasn't sure what was happening," he replied. "How long were you standing there?" Rose asked.

"I don't know. Long enough. I couldn't leave after seeing you," he said, now looking at her with an intense gaze. Rose looked at him and then turned and looked in the other direction. "I'm sorry you had to see that," Rose said, as she stood up.

Denver stood up and grabbed her by her arms. He pulled her to him and began to kiss her. Rose fought him at first but Denver held her tight. Rose tried to push away, but then just as quickly, stopped fighting and began to kiss him back.

Denver moved her toward the wall grabbed both her legs and began to fuck her against the wall. He was strong.

He had stamina and was passionate like Boston. Rose fucked him back. She totally gave in to him and was enjoying him. He was huge like his brother and he showed her no mercy. Denver pushed her head to the side and sucked her neck so hard that he put a hickey right under her ear.

"Stop Denver. We can't" she said. "Too late," he replied. Long after she had an orgasm, he was still holding her and fucking. Rose began to fear getting caught and was ready for him to stop. She whispered to him, "We need to stop." Denver continued, whispering in her ear, "No. I can't."

Denver put her legs down, pulled her to the floor and fucked her doggystyle for another twenty-five minutes before pulling out and coming all over her ass. After laying on the floor for a few minutes, he tried to kiss her but she turned away. "Just go," she said, looking emotional and wracked with guilt. He tried holding her and she pushed his hands away. Denver got up and walked to one of the bathrooms off the theater room. He shut the door and stood there motionless.

What have I done? Damn! And I still want to fuck her. Boston's going to kill me. He can never know about this. Denver came out of the bathroom and walked up to Rose. "Rose. Please don't tell Boston," he said. "Tell him what?" she replied.

Chapter Nine – Full Circle

*T*he warm bath was just what the doctor ordered for an exhausted Rose. She had a lot to think about. She felt as though she was spiraling out of control and she had no one to turn to. *What is wrong with me? Did I just fuck Denver?* Rose laid back in the tub and rinsed her vagina walls as if she were washing away the seven deadly sins. She soaked for hours. Tears streamed down her face as she sat there dreading the arrival of Boston the next morning. Boston was flying back early after a successful business trip. Rose wasn't sure she could even look him in his face. She knew that she could get emotional easily and feared that the sight of him may provoke her to tears. Rose put her pajamas on and went down to the first floor. She thought she heard something in the kitchen and went to take a look.

Denver was standing at the sink drinking a glass of water. "Denver. What are you doing here? Boston's on his way back," she said nervously. "I needed to see you one more time before he gets here," Denver said. Rose was attracted to him and knew she had to get him out of the house. "No. No. Leave please," she insisted, as she shook her head at him. Denver grabbed her and started kissing her. "You smell good," he whispered in her ear. Rose pushed him away and walked toward the stairs. "I'm going upstairs and you're leaving. This is not right. Let yourself out Denver. You have to go," she said. Denver sat down on the stairs and cupped his hands on his forehead. He knew he would never get the chance to be with her again and since they had already crossed the line, he wanted her again. Denver went up the stairs and grabbed Rose. "It's too late Rose. I promise to stay away after this," he insisted. "No you won't! Denver please! We can't," she replied. Rose paused. She desired him. Boston wasn't due back until the next day. "One more time then you stay away from me," she pleaded. "I promise," he said.

Denver made several calls on his way home from his brother's house. He called his brother Bronx and when he didn't answer he called Chicago. Chicago didn't pick up either and Denver hung up and drove to a topless bar that he frequented. He was sweating and stressed out about what he had done. He wanted to confide in one of his older brothers about it.

Bronx was rational and could keep a secret. He knew of other indiscretions Denver got himself involved in and had never told anyone. Denver trusted Bronx's wisdom and advice. His brother Chicago was trustworthy as well and was the peacemaker in the family. He would go out of his way to set things straight and he understood Denver's weaknesses. Chicago was just like Denver when he was a young gentleman. But he had become a much more responsible man as he got older. Denver had slept with Chicago's wife before they got married and Chicago had forgiven him. He tried Bronx again.

"Hello," Bronx answered.

"Hey man, it's Den. You busy?" he asked.

"Not at the moment. What's going on?" Bronx replied.

"I need to see you," Denver stated.

"Can it wait?" he asked.

"No it can't. Come to the Nile. I need to talk to you," Denver cautioned.

"Why there?" Bronx asked.

"Cause I need a drink," he replied.

"Is it that bad?" he asked, in a worried tone.

"Yeah. It is."

Bronx went to his wife, told her he had an emergency and kissed her bye before heading to *The Nile*. When he got there, he spotted Denver immediately. Denver was sitting at the bar, holding a shot glass in his hand and looking distraught. Bronx walked up and sat down next to him. "Let me get a Hennessey on the rocks please," Bronx asked the waiter, as he sat next to his brother. "Talk to me Den. What's going on?" he said to his obviously troubled brother.

Denver took the shot of Patron and then ordered another one. He sat there silent, looking at his reflection in the mirror behind the bar. "Damn. Are you serious," Bronx stressed. "Please don't say what I think you're going to say. Is this about the woman making claims that you grabbed her a few months ago?" Bronx asked.

Denver looked at his brother with surprise. "No. I never fucked her," he said. "That's not what she said," Bronx replied. "I let her suck my dick. Once. But that was a long time ago. No, nothing like that," he said. "Then what is it?"

Bronx asked. Denver paused, still reluctant to speak about it. "Den. You called me. I'm here. Talk to me," Bronx urged. "I slipped up with Boston's girl," he said, refusing to look Bronx in the eyes. Bronx stood up off the chair in shock. "What! What did you say? Slipped as in fucked?" he asked. Denver shook his head. "No. Man naw. Tell me you didn't fucking do that. Denver! You did not do that," Bronx stressed as he shook his head in disbelief.

Bronx sat back down and tried to calm himself. "Denver, listen to me," he said, as he thought carefully about what he wanted to say. Bronx paused to weigh his words because it was obvious to him Denver was a wreck. "You have got to get some kind of control over your dick. You cannot do these types of things and especially to your brothers. We're adults with families now. You had a family and you destroyed it for this very reason. When will you learn," he urged. Bronx was growing frustrated of his younger brothers careless and selfish decisions. He worried that it would hurt the family. Boston could be unforgiving and was known to hold grudges for extended periods of time. Bronx knew he had to do damage control but he wasn't sure how.

Bronx started rubbing his head, something he did when he got nervous. "This will destroy him. He's in love with that woman. He got plans for her. This is messed up man. You need to wait, get your head on straight and find the time to tell him," he stated. Bronx stood up, took his shot of Hennessey, pat his brother on the back and walked out.

*I*t was the middle of the night and Rose tossed and turned as she tried to get some sleep. By morning, she hadn't slept and was exhausted. She arose and went to the bathroom to shower. *What the hell is that. Oh no. Why did he do that? What is wrong with him?* Rose was upset to see that Denver had put a hickey on her neck. She scrambled to find something to cover it with. She didn't wear makeup and she didn't have much time. *I need to find a 24-hour drug store. This is insane. I have to cover this,* she thought.

Rose threw on some clothes and drove in the heavy snow, in search of a drug store. She drove several miles before she finally saw one and got what she needed. She'd made it back home and was dressed and ready for Boston. Rose could see the car coming down the driveway. She was so nervous that she started to cry. *Shit!* She ran to look in the mirror and wiped her eyes as Boston was walking through the front door. Rose wiped her face and ran out of the bathroom and down the stairs. "Hey baby," she said, as she walked up to him. Boston was all smiles. He missed her. Rose went to him and hugged and kissed him. Boston greeted her.

"Hi baby. I missed you. You got up for me. This is kind of early for you," he said. "I missed you. I couldn't sleep," she replied, as Boston grabbed his bags and headed to his room. Rose sat on the bed, and told Boston about her days as he unpacked. She was still nervous from her tryst with Denver and tried to keep her composure. She constantly thought of the mark on her neck and tried to keep her body angled in a way, so he wouldn't see anything. "Take that off," Boston said, looking at her with lust. He was ready to be with her and he wanted her at that moment. Rose made love to Boston all day and into the night that evening, as she tried to forget about Denver. She was relieved and happy to have him back home. She couldn't help but be consumed with guilt. *Rose! What have you done?*

*****

"I'm coming down the street. I'll be there in a minute," Raleigh said, as she drove down the street. Boston's younger sister was on her way to visit with Rose and get something to eat later in the day. As she approached the home, she saw his neighbor Jennifer, standing outside working on her garden. "Hey Jenn," Raleigh said as she waved.

Jennifer knew the family well. She was the young wife of a prominent Attorney and her and Raleigh had become friends over the years. "Raleigh. Where have you been? I haven't seen you in a while," she asked. "I've been around. I'm remodeling my salon. I'm turning it into a day spa and salon. I had to buy the building next door and then we started tearing the walls down. It's a lot," Raleigh replied. "Oh, wow. Well let me know when it's complete. I need some pampering," Jenn said.

As the conversation went on, Jennifer mentioned Denver. She'd had a crush on Denver for years and liked flirting with him. He usually flirted back at the pretty brunette with ocean blue colored eyes and infectious smile. She hadn't seen much of him since Rose had moved in. "I saw Denver last weekend. I thought he saw me but he just took off. Has he been ok?" Jenn asked.

"Yeah. He's good. You saw him here? Over Boston's house?" Raleigh asked.

"Yeah. Last Saturday and Sunday," Jenn replied. Raleigh looked perplexed. *Boston wasn't here last weekend*, she thought.

"Well let me go. Rose is waiting for me." Raleigh noted.

The women waved to each other and Raleigh pulled up into Boston's driveway. Before she got out of the car, Raleigh called her sister Tacoma.

"Hey what you doing?" she said, as she sat there.

"Nothing at the moment. What about you? Where you at?" Tacoma asked.

"I'm over Boston's. Me and Rose supposed to go eat later. Um…Listen…Wasn't Boston out of town last weekend?" she asked.

"Yeah. Why?" Tacoma replied.

"Cause Jenn across the street said she saw Denver here Saturday and Sunday," Raleigh said in a low voice. She was sure Tacoma was just seconds from flying off the handle if she was thinking the same thing. Something was wrong with that scenario.

The sisters didn't say anything for a few seconds. It was apparent to Raleigh that Tacoma thought there was foul play. Denver was a notorious womanizer and Tacoma had already suspected that he was attracted to Rose. She had caught a few inappropriate stares from Denver as Rose talked to Raleigh one night while at their brothers' lounge. "Let me call you back Raleigh," she said.

Tacoma got in her car and called her brother. She knew he was home because she had just spoken to him. Denver picked up after several rings.

"Hey," he said.

"Hey. I'm on my way. I need to talk to you," Tacoma said.

"What about?" Denver asked.

"I'll tell you. I'm almost there," she replied and hung up. Tacoma loved her brothers and she'd played mediator between them before. But this was on a different level. She knew this could tear them apart and she wanted to do damage control. She could see Denver standing in his window looking out as she pulled into the parking space. She got out and looked up and waved. Denver buzzed her in.

"Hey," she said, as she walked past her brother. "Hey Tae. What's wrong?" he asked.

"Everything. So I'm just going to come out and say it. What happened last weekend and don't lie to me cause I know." Denver looked at Tacoma. He didn't know what she knew, but he was sure Bronx hadn't said anything. That would be totally out of character for him. Tacoma was careful not to let on that she really didn't know anything.

"I don't know what you mean," Denver said, his voice cracking as he hesitated.

"Denver. You look so fucking guilty right now. You fucked her didn't you?" she said, as she got teary eyed. Tacoma hated family betrayal. She was always working hard to keep the family close and bonded. If he had fucked Rose, then that was the ultimate betrayal and one that would cause a rift between them.

Denver walked away from Tacoma looking down and biting his lip in fear. He didn't want Boston to find out. But he was backed into a corner and believing that Rose possibly told her, decided to confess. "Yes," he said. "What? How could you do that," she said, crying, as she got in her brothers' face. "How could you do that to him? He's going to be devastated. He will never forgive you," she said, as she walked away from him. Denver walked closer to his sister.

"You can't tell him Tay," he said.

"I'm not. But that sort of thing doesn't stay hidden. It's going to come out Denver. I'm not telling him. You're going to tell him," she asserted.

"I'm not telling him that. Ever!" Denver yelled.

"You have to. He needs to know what kind of bitch he got living with him," she warned.

"No. I can't," he replied. Tacoma stormed out of Denver condo, furious and inconsolable.

Tacoma called Raleigh in tears. Raleigh listened as Tacoma ranted and made threats toward Rose. Raleigh walked towards the great room as Rose looked on. Rose assumed Raleigh just needed privacy for the call and thought nothing of it. Raleigh hung up from Tacoma and told Rose she had to make a quick run and she would call her in a minute.

Raleigh called Tacoma back urging her not to come to Boston's house. "Tacoma. Don't come here and jump on this girl. You can't do that. Where are you?" she asked.

"She's no good Raleigh. She's fucking her ex. She's been fucking Denver. I'm not letting my brother go out like that," Tacoma said.

"But it's going to cause beef between him and Denver," Raleigh said, concerned for her brother's safety.

"Denver should have thought of that before he went over there, not once but twice. I don't feel sorry for him. He's so ungrateful. He thinks he can do whatever and have whomever he wants with no consequences," Tacoma ranted.

"He did this same shit to Chicago. Remember?" she said, as angry at her brother's lack of respect.

"That was a long time ago Tae," Raleigh replied.

"Obviously not Raleigh. The shit is still happening. Besides, this isn't about Denver. I'm trying to protect Boston. I'll tell dad first so he can help calm Boston down. But Boston needs to know," Tacoma replied.

****

It was quiet for the next few weeks. Tacoma was hanging around Boston a lot more and showing up at his office regularly. He believed she was there out of boredom and needed something to do. Tacoma had worked there before, a few years back and she knew her way around. She was good at marketing and had begun pitching ideas to the staff. Tacoma was still angry at Denver and had only spoken to him a few times since their conversation about Rose.

Rose was keeping a low profile and staying close to home. She could feel the tension in the air. Tacoma didn't return any of her calls and Raleigh was vague and always claiming to be too busy to hang out. Boston stepped out of his office and walked up to his other secretary Maria.

"Can you get me a table for two over at *Wellington's*. Make it for four o'clock?" he asked.

"Sure Mr. St. Rock," Maria replied. Boston went over to the Marketing Office where Tacoma was to check in on her. He liked having her around more. He loved family to work with him. He trusted family and would always rather have family around than strangers. He was generous with his family and it made him feel needed.

"Hey. How's it going?" Boston said.

"Good. Adding some more key points to the PowerPoint presentation I created for Mr. Weiss," Tacoma replied.

"Oh ok. Don't let me disturb you then. I'm leaving soon. Rose is coming here. We're going to eat at Wellington's," Boston said. Tacoma looked at him and then looked back at her computer.

"Ok," she replied.

Boston shut her door and Tacoma stopped typing. She was furious. She hadn't seen or talked to Rose. And she was growing anxious to expose what she knew about her. But she loved both of her brothers and this could tear them apart. Denver was Boston's right hand man and a vital part of the company. If he and Boston were to fall out, how would Boston maintain. There was a level of quality and detail that went into making their ideas a reality. Boston was the creative one who came up with the ideas and Denver made it happen. Their working dynamic made *Rockwater* the powerhouse company that it was.

Tacoma continued working for the next several minutes. She had tweaked her PowerPoint and was ready to leave. She didn't want to be there when Rose arrived. She was feeling an overwhelming amount of stress and needed to speak to someone. As she prepared to go, she decided to call her older sister Aurora. Aurora was the wise one. She was stable, married and had four children. Aurora was the "nurturing mom" type, always present and there for her family when they needed her. Tacoma hadn't told Aurora. She hadn't said anything to anyone except Raleigh.

Aurora answered and Tacoma spoke with her just for a minute. Before she could go into what happened with

Denver and Rose, she heard a familiar voice. "Hey. I have to call you back," she said to her sister. Tacoma ended her called and opened her office door so she could hear the person a little better. She could hear the faint and soft-spoken voice that sounded familiar. *That's her. She's here!*

Tacoma grabbed her keys and walked out into the main lobby. Rose stood there and smiled when she saw Tacoma approaching. Roses' smile quickly turned to a look of concern as Tacoma approached her. She could see that Tacoma was upset about something and Tacoma was approaching fast. "What's wrong," Rose asked. "You're what's wrong. I know all about you and Denver. How dare you fuck my brother Denver. I guess you plan on fucking all ten of them you slut," Tacoma seethed. Rose shook her head *no* which infuriated Tacoma.

Tacoma began hitting Rose in the face. She slapped her and grabbed her by the hair and began hitting her in the head. Rose tried to fight back but Tacoma was too strong. Tacoma swung, hitting Rose on the top of her head and on the side of her face. She was unremitting, and several people tried to break it up but Tacoma continued. Maria ran over and broke them up.

"Tacoma. Stop! Don't do this here. What is going on," she asked. Tacoma stared at Rose. Rose stood there in shock holding her face and crying as Tacoma just glared at her. She wanted to get at her again, but she respected Maria and didn't want her to get hurt in the process. Rose walked away and hurried toward Boston's office and closed the door. Tacoma stood with Maria as Maria tried to calm her down. She called Rose names but was careful not to tell Boston's business. She didn't leave. She was waiting on Boston to return. She knew she would need to explain the *ass whoopin* she had just inflicted upon Rose.

Rose was panicked. She was afraid to leave out of Boston's office. She tried calling Boston, but got no answer. She knew Tacoma was still furious and she didn't want to encounter her again. *Where is Boston? How does she know? Damn you Denver,* she thought, as she paced the floor. Rose was getting desperate. She needed someone to come get her. She didn't want to call the police and get Boston's sister in trouble. *I'll call Ashley. I don't have a choice. She may come get me if she doesn't hate me now.*

Rose called Ashley. Ashley grew up the only girl in a house with three older brothers. She was fearless and had defended Rose many times in the past.

"Hello," Ashley answered.

"Ashley can you come get me? I'm in trouble." Rose pleaded.

"What? What kind of trouble?" Ashley replied.

"Boston's sister just jumped on me," Rose said, as she wept uncontrollably.

"What! I'm on my way. Where are you?" she asked. Ashley had been protective of Rose since they were young girls. There was always issues with girls and their boyfriends with regards to Rose. And Ashley had fought her battles more than a few times.

"I'm at Boston's office, but he's not here. I can't stay here. She's still mad and she's still here," Rose replied. Rose hung up from Ashley and tried to call Boston again but he still wasn't answering. Rose looked over on his bookcase and saw his phone sitting there on the charger. *Dammit! His phone is here.*

She could hear Tacoma on her cell phone ranting about her. *I've got to get out of here*, she thought, as she wiped her eyes. After what seemed like an eternity, Rose looked out the window and saw a car pull up. To her surprise, Tina got out of the passenger side and Ashley exited from the driver's side. Rose was relieved to see Ashley but wondered what Tina was doing there. *Ashley called Tina!*

The two women entered the office and it was clear to everyone standing around, that they weren't there to talk. Tina walked up to the women standing around. "Which one of you is Tacoma?" she asked. The women had been talking about what happened and had rallied around Tacoma in an effort to calm the situation. Tacoma, still reeling from the events said, "I am."

Tina immediately and without warning, walked over to Tacoma and started punching her in the face. As the other women tried to intervene Tina would turn on them. She would then return, punching, slapping and kicking Tacoma. Tacoma tried to keep up but she was no match for Tina. She was a skilled fighter. She had been in way too many street brawls over the years for Tacoma to stand a chance. Boston and Bronx walked through the door, shocked at the fight that was happening in the middle of the lobby. They walked over to the women and broke up the fight. Boston pulled Tina away.

"Who the fuck are you? You better leave here now," Boston said, furious. Tacoma tried to lunge for Tina but

Bronx held her back. "What's going on Tacoma?" Bronx asked. Tacoma just stood there with a blank stare.

Rose had come out of Boston's office and was standing there watching in fear. But was relieved that Tina was there. She just stared at Tina. But when Tina looked back at her daughter, Rose nodded in affirmation. It was the first time she had ever felt protected by her mother. Rose couldn't bear to look at Boston as she stood there wracked with guilt. Tina smiled at Rose and then turned to Tacoma.

"If you ever touch my daughter again, I will fucking kill you," Tina warned.

"Who are you talking about?" Boston asked.

"Rosalee," replied Tina. Boston looked at Rose then turned his attention to Tacoma.

"You hit Rose?" he asked.

"Yeah, I did," Tacoma replied.

"Why would you do that?" Boston asked. Tacoma paused, looked at Rose then looked backed at Boston.

"She fucked Denver. That's why," she replied.

Boston was silent for a moment. He wasn't sure he heard her right. He stood and stared at Rose with such a glare that Tina became uncomfortable. She walked up to her daughter and took her by the hand. Boston stood there in disbelief. Staring at Rose. Wanting to grab her. Wanting an explanation. Questioning who she was as a woman. His mind raced and for the first time, he was at a loss for words. Everyone standing around was in shock. Some of the women walked away and went back to their offices. Bronx walked up to Boston and placed his hand on his shoulder.

"Come on. Just let them leave," he urged. Rose was leaving and Boston followed her out with Bronx close behind.

"I want to talk to you now Rose," he said, walking quickly to catch up to her. She looked at him with tears in her eyes.

"I can't. I gotta go right now," she said, as she continued to walk fast, hoping to distance herself from the situation. Boston grabbed Roses' arm and Tina jerked his hand away.

"I will call the police and this will turn into something else. Do you want that?" she said.

"I know you're mad right now, but you need to calm down first. Everyone needs to calm down. She'll talk to you when she's ready," Tina insisted. The three women got into Ashley's car and pulled off. Boston stood outside his office watching the car as it sped down the street. Bronx stood next to him trying to console his younger brother.

"Let's go have a drink and talk," Bronx urged.

"No, I need to talk to Denver. Now!"

The drive to Roses' home was uneventful. Ashley and Tina tried to get Rose to talk about what had happened, but she was too distraught. She sat in the back seat staring out the window. Tina looked back at Rose.

"You want to come stay with me?" she asked. "No. I have my own house," Rose replied. "The old house you used to live in?" Tina asked.

"Yeah. I brought it from that lady years ago and I fixed it up. Take me there," she said. Ashley smiled at Rose in the rear-view mirror as Rose lay her head back on the seat. She smiled at Ashley and looked out the window.

Rose spotted a pile of furniture in front of an old remodeled building and asked Ashley to stop. She had noticed an oil painting of what appeared to be a little girl and wanted to get a closer look. Ashley pulled over and Rose got out and grabbed the painting.

"What's that?" Ashley asked.

"A beautiful painting. I'm going to hang this on my wall," she said. It was a picture of a little girl in a rain coat dancing in the rain.

The picture made Rose feel warm, happy and safe. She didn't want to think about the events that had just occurred. Her life had turned upside down and she didn't know what the future held. Rose thought of Boston and wondered if he hated her. She thought of Denver and wondered why he would take such a risk. She even thought of Max and wondered if he still loved her. The only people at the moment, she had in her life that she knew loved her was her mother and her best friend. Rose closed her eyes and relaxed for the rest of the ride home.

Tina was shocked when she saw the house as they were coming up the driveway. "Oh my Rose. It looks totally different. It's beautiful. Where did you get the money to get it looking like that?" Tina asked.

"Max and Boston," she replied nonchalantly, as she tried to pull herself together. Rose was a quiet wreck. She had just loss her best friend. The love of her life. The man she was in love with. She knew Boston would never forgive her and she felt unworthy of him. Tina walked to the house with Rose and hugged her when they got on the porch.

"You call me Rose if you need me. I'm serious. I got you. I love you," she said, looking at her daughter and trying to read her emotionless facial expression.

Rose hugged Tina and waved bye to Ashley. "You want me to stay with you for a while? I can if you need me to," Tina stated.

"No. I'm ok now. I'm just tired and hungry," she replied.

"Sleepy and hungry! Rose, get a pregnancy test when you get a chance," Tina said, as she was walking to the car. Rose opened the door and then waved as the car pulled off. She entered her newly renovated home, took a deep breath and exhaled.

"Welcome home," she said as her voice trembled. It was hard keeping a straight face in front of her mother and Ashley. The brave front was a façade. She was broken and ready to break down. It was ironic she was back where she started. Like a bad dream. Rose fell slowly to the floor. What happened wasn't supposed to happen.

"I have to get him back! How could I... How could this...No!" she shouted, as tears rolled down her cheeks. Rose wiped her eyes and gathered her composure. Her life had turned chaotic because she had done things. Terrible things. And it had cost her the man she loved. Rose looked out the window. She saw the tail end of a white Mercedes drive by. She furrowed then looked off. A thought occurred to her. Boston, even though he had a white Mercedes, did not know where she lived. Still a Mercedes driving in her low-income neighborhood was not a typical everyday sight either. Rose stood hoping the car turned around. She watched as the car turned the corner. Rose exhaled sharply.

He will come for me, she thought as she walked away. She could only hope he would. One day.

Please leave a Review for the book! Thank you for your support!

Your support is appreciated!

Smokey Moment

More Books By

Smokey Moment

Standalones

The Twin

Her Sister's Husband

Wreckless

Everything I Want

Secrets, Lies & Video

Keeping Him Quiet

Gifted

Through The Wires

Beauty is Sleeping

Baby Girl

His Many Wives

Two-part Sagas, Series or Trilogies:

Ways of Kings I

Ways of Kings II

Stray I

Stray II New Life

Stray III Covenant

Rocks and Stones Between a Rose Part I

Rocks and Stones Between a Rose Part II

Pretty Fin

Pretty Fin II

Made in the USA
Monee, IL
27 April 2021